DANNY
THE CHAMPION OF
THE WORLD

*More fun and excitement from
that master storyteller, Roald Dahl.*

"A daring and hilarious adventure story."

—*Memphis Press Scimitar*

"Roald Dahl has created a whole array of fascinating characters...An imaginative and entertaining story."

—*Booklist*

"The story progresses rapidly and intriguingly, but its main value is in the portrayal of the kind of relationship between two people that makes life worthwhile—mutual respect, concern, and sharing of work and play."

—*School Library Journal*

"Sentimental, escapist humor at its delicious best. Children will adore the bravery and zaniness of Danny and Dad."

—Council on Interracial Books for Children

"A fast-moving, light-hearted romp that leaves the reader with a warm, cozy feeling."

—Association of Children's Librarians

DANNY
The Champion of the World

❧

ROALD DAHL

ILLUSTRATED BY JILL BENNETT

A BANTAM SKYLARK BOOK®
TORONTO • NEW YORK • LONDON • SYDNEY • AUCKLAND

This low-priced Bantam Book
has been completely reset in a type face
designed for easy reading, and was printed
from new plates. It contains the complete
text of the original hard-cover edition.
NOT ONE WORD HAS BEEN OMITTED.

RL 5, 009-013

DANNY THE CHAMPION OF THE WORLD

A Bantam Skylark Book / published by arrangement with
Alfred A. Knopf, Inc.

PRINTING HISTORY

Knopf edition published September 1975
2nd printing . . . . May 1976
3rd printing . . . December 1977

Bantam Skylark edition / October 1978

2nd printing . . . . June 1979	5th printing . . . . February 1981
3rd printing . . . . July 1979	6th printing . . . . . . August 1981
4th printing . . . . June 1980	7th printing . . . . . October 1982

ISBN 0-553-15196-7

Published simultaneously in the United States and Canada

Bantam Books are published by Bantam Books, Inc. Its trademark, consisting of the words "Bantam Books" and the portrayal of a rooster, is Registered in U.S. Patent and Trademark
Office and in other countries. Marca Registrada. Bantam
Books, Inc., 666 Fifth Avenue, New York, New York 10103.

PRINTED IN THE UNITED STATES OF AMERICA

16   15   14   13   12   11   10   9   8

This book is for the whole family

PAT

TESSA

THEO

OPHELIA

LUCY

Contents

❧

DANNY
The Champion of the World

❧

1

∾

The Filling Station

WHEN I WAS four months old, my mother died suddenly and my father was left to look after me all by himself. This is how I looked at the time.

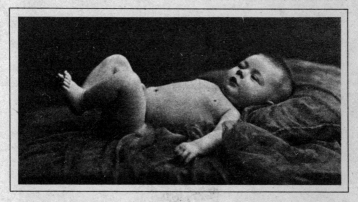

I had no brothers or sisters.

So all through my boyhood, from the age of four months onward, there was just us two, my father and me.

We lived in an old gypsy caravan behind a filling station. My father owned the filling station and the caravan and a small meadow behind, but that was about all he owned in the world. It was a very small filling station on a small country road surrounded by fields and woody hills.

While I was still a baby, my father washed me and fed me and changed my diapers and did all the millions of other things a mother normally does for her child. That is not an easy task for a man, especially when he has to earn his living at the same time by repairing automobile engines and serving customers with gasoline.

But my father didn't seem to mind. I think that all the love he had felt for my mother when she was alive he now lavished upon me. During my early years, I never had a moment's unhappiness or illness, and here I am on my fifth birthday.

I was now a scruffy little boy as you can see, with grease and oil all over me, but that was because I spent all day in the workshop helping my father with the automobiles.

The filling station itself had only two pumps. There was a wooden shed behind the pumps that served as an office. There was nothing in the office except an old table and a cash register to put the money into. It was one of those where you pressed a button and a bell rang and the drawer shot out with a terrific bang. I used to love that.

The square brick building to the right of the office was the workshop. My father built that himself with loving care, and it was the only really solid thing on the place. "We are engineers, you and I," he used to say to me. "We earn our living by repairing engines and we can't do good work in a rotten workshop." It was a fine workshop, big enough to take one automobile comfortably and leave plenty of room around the sides for working. It had a telephone so that customers could ring up and arrange to bring their cars in for repair.

The caravan was our house and our home. It was a real old gypsy wagon with big wheels and fine patterns painted all over it in yellow and red and blue. My father said it was at least one hundred and fifty years old. Many gypsy children, he said, had been born in it and had grown up within its wooden walls. With a horse to pull it, the old caravan must have wandered for thousands of miles along the roads and lanes of England. But now its wanderings were over, and because the wooden spokes in the wheels were beginning to rot, my father had propped it up underneath with bricks.

There was only one room in the caravan, and it wasn't much bigger than a fair-sized modern bathroom. It was a

narrow room, the shape of the caravan itself, and against the back wall were two bunk beds, one above the other. The top one was my father's, the bottom one mine.

Although we had electric lights in the workshop, we were not allowed to have them in the caravan. The electricity people said it was unsafe to put wires into something as old and rickety as that. So we got our heat and light in much the same way as the gypsies had done years ago. There was a wood-burning stove with a chimney that went up through the roof, and this kept us warm in winter. There was a kerosene burner on which to boil a kettle or cook a stew, and there was a kerosene lamp hanging from the ceiling.

When I needed a bath, my father would heat a kettle of water and pour it into a basin. Then he would strip me naked and scrub me all over, standing up. This, I think, got me just as clean as if I were washed in a bathtub—probably cleaner because I didn't finish up sitting in my own dirty water.

For furniture, we had two chairs and a small table, and those, apart from a tiny chest of drawers, were all the home comforts we possessed. They were all we needed.

The lavatory was a funny little wooden hut standing in the meadow way back of the caravan. It was fine in summertime, but I can tell you that sitting out there on a snowy day in winter was like sitting in an icebox.

Immediately behind the caravan was an old apple tree. It bore fine apples that ripened in the middle of September. You could go on picking them for the next four or five weeks. Some of the boughs of the tree hung right over the caravan and when the wind blew the apples down in the night, they often landed on our roof. I would hear them going *thump* . . . *thump* . . . *thump* . . . above my head as I lay in my bunk, but those noises never frightened me because I knew exactly what was making them.

I really loved living in that gypsy caravan. I loved it especially in the evenings when I was tucked up in my bunk and my father was telling me stories. The kerosene lamp was turned low, and I could see lumps of wood glowing red-hot in the old stove, and wonderful it was to be lying there snug and warm in my bunk in that little room. Most wonderful of all was the feeling that when I went to sleep, my father would still be there, very close to me, sitting in his chair by the fire, or lying in the bunk above my own.

2

The Big Friendly Giant

MY FATHER, WITHOUT the slightest doubt, was the most marvelous and exciting father any boy ever had. Here is a picture of him.

You might think, if you didn't know him well, that he was a stern and serious man. He wasn't. He was actually a wildly funny person. What made him appear so serious was the fact that he never smiled with his mouth. He did it all with his eyes. He had brilliant blue eyes and when he thought of something funny, his eyes would flash and, if you looked carefully, you could actually see a tiny little golden spark dancing in the middle of each eye. But the mouth never moved.

I was glad my father was an eye-smiler. It meant he never gave me a fake smile because it's impossible to make your eyes twinkle if you aren't feeling twinkly yourself. A mouth-smile is different. You can fake a mouth-smile any time you want, simply by moving your lips. I've also learned that a real mouth-smile always has an eye-smile to go with it. So watch out, I say, when someone smiles at you with his mouth but his eyes stay the same. It's sure to be a phony.

My father was not what you would call an educated man. I doubt he had read twenty books in his life. But he was a marvelous storyteller. He used to make up a bedtime story for me every single night, and the best ones were turned into serials and went on for many nights running.

One of them, which must have gone on for at least fifty nights, was about an enormous fellow called "The Big Friendly Giant," or "The BFG" for short. The BFG was three times as tall as an ordinary man and his hands were as big as wheelbarrows. He lived in a vast underground cavern not far from our filling station and he only came out into the open when it was dark. Inside the cavern he had a powder factory where he made more than one hundred different kinds of magic powder.

Occasionally, as he told his stories, my father would stride up and down waving his arms and waggling his fingers. But most times he would sit close to me on the edge of my bunk and speak very softly.

"The Big Friendly Giant makes his magic powders out of the dreams that children dream when they are asleep," he said.

"How?" I asked. "Tell me how, dad."

"Dreams, my love, are very mysterious things. They float around in the night air like little clouds, searching for sleeping people."

"Can you see them?" I asked.

"Nobody can see them."

"Then how does The Big Friendly Giant catch them?"

"Ah," my father said, "that is the interesting part. A dream, you see, as it goes drifting through the night air, makes a tiny little buzzing-humming sound, a sound so soft and low it is impossible for ordinary people to hear it. But The BFG can hear it easily. His sense of hearing is absolutely fantastic."

I loved the intent look on my father's face when he was telling a story. His face was pale and still and distant, unconscious of everything around him.

"The BFG," he said, "can hear the tread of a ladybug's footsteps as she walks across a leaf. He can hear the whisperings of ants as they scurry around in the soil talking to one another. He can hear the sudden shrill cry of pain a tree gives out when a woodman cuts into it with an ax. Ah yes, my darling, there is a whole world of sound around us that we cannot hear because our ears are simply not sensitive enough."

"What happens when he catches the dreams?" I asked.

"He imprisons them in glass bottles and screws the tops down tight," my father said. "He has thousands of these bottles in his cave."

"Does he catch bad dreams as well as good ones?"

"Yes," my father said. "He catches both. But he only uses the good ones in his powders."

"What does he do with the bad ones?"

"He explodes them."

It is impossible to tell you how much I loved my father. When he was sitting close to me on my bunk I would reach out and slide my hand into his, and then he would fold his long fingers around my fist, holding it tight.

"What does The BFG do with his powders after he has made them?" I asked.

"In the dead of night," my father said, "he goes prowling through the villages searching for houses where children are asleep. Because of his great height he can reach windows that are two and even three flights up, and when he finds a room with a sleeping child, he opens his suitcase—"

"His suitcase?" I said.

"The BFG always carries a suitcase and a blowpipe," my father said. "The blowpipe is as long as a lamppost. The suitcase is for the powders. So he opens the suitcase and selects exactly the right powder—and he puts it into the blowpipe—and he slides the blowpipe in through the open

window—and poof!—he blows in the powder—and the powder floats around the room—and the child breathes it in—"

"And then what?" I asked.

"And then, Danny, the child begins to dream a marvelous and fantastic dream—and when the dream reaches its most marvelous and fantastic moment—then the magic powder really takes over—and suddenly the dream is not a dream any longer but a real happening—and the child is not asleep in bed—he is fully awake and is actually in the place of the dream and is taking part in the whole thing—I mean really taking part—in real life. More about that tomorrow. It's getting late. Good night, Danny. Go to sleep."

My father kissed me and then he turned down the wick of the little kerosene lamp until the flame went out. He seated himself in front of the wood stove which now made a lovely red glow in the darkroom.

"Dad," I whispered.

"What is it?"

"Have you ever actually seen The Big Friendly Giant?"

"Once," my father said. "Only once."

"You did! Where?"

"I was out behind the caravan," my father said, "and it was a clear moonlit night, and I happened to look up and suddenly I saw this tremendous tall person running along the crest of the hill. He had a queer long-striding lolloping gait and his black cloak was streaming out behind him like the wings of a bird. There was a big suitcase in one hand and a blowpipe in the other, and when he came to the high hawthorne hedge at the end of the field, he just strode over it as though it wasn't there."

"Were you frightened, dad?"

"No," my father said. "It was thrilling to see him, and a little eerie, but I wasn't frightened. Go to sleep now. Good night."

3

Cars and Kites and Fire Balloons

MY FATHER WAS A fine mechanic. People who lived miles away used to bring their automobiles to him for repair rather than take them to their nearest garage. He loved engines. "A gasoline engine is sheer magic," he said to me once. "Just imagine being able to take a thousand different bits of metal—and if you fit them all together in a certain way—and then if you feed them a little oil and gasoline—and if you press a little switch—suddenly those bits of metal will all come to life—and they will purr and hum and roar—they will make the wheels of a motor car go whizzing around at fantastic speeds. . . ."

It was inevitable that I, too, should fall in love with engines and automobiles. Don't forget that even before I could walk, the workshop had been my playroom, for where else could my father have put me so that he could keep an eye on me all day long? My toys were the greasy cogs and springs and pistons that lay around all over the place, and these, I can promise you, were far more fun to play with than most of the plastic rubbish children are given nowadays.

So almost from birth, I began training to be a mechanic.

But now that I was five years old, there was the problem of school to think about. It was the law that parents must send their children to school at the age of five, and my father knew about this.

We were in the workshop, I remember, on my fifth birthday, when the talk about school started. I was helping my father to fit new brake linings to the rear wheel of a big Ford when suddenly he said to me, "You know something interesting, Danny? You must be easily the best five-year-old mechanic in the world."

This was the greatest compliment he had ever paid me. I was enormously pleased.

"You like this work, don't you?" he said. "All this messing about with engines."

"I absolutely love it," I said.

He turned and faced me and laid a hand gently on my shoulder. "I want to teach you to be a great mechanic," he said. "And when you grow up, I hope you will become a

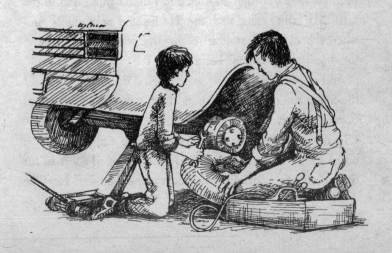

famous designing engineer, a man who designs new and better engines for automobiles and airplanes. For that," he added, "you will need a really good education. But I don't want to send you to school quite yet. In another two years you will have learned enough here with me to be able to take a small engine completely to pieces and put it together again all by yourself. After that, you can go to school."

You probably think my father was crazy trying to teach a young child to be an expert mechanic, but as a matter of fact he wasn't crazy at all. I learned fast and I loved every moment of it. And luckily for us, nobody came knocking on the door to ask why I wasn't attending school.

So two more years went by, and at the age of seven, believe it or not, I really could take a small engine to pieces and put it together again. I mean properly to pieces, pistons and crankshaft and all. The time had come to start school.

My school was in the nearest village, two miles away. We didn't have a car of our own. We couldn't afford one. But the walk took only half an hour and I didn't mind that in the least. My father came with me. He insisted on coming. And when school ended at four in the afternoon, he was always there waiting to walk me home.

And so life went on. The world I lived in consisted only of the filling station, the workshop, the caravan, the school, and of course the woods and meadows and streams in the country-side around. But I was never bored. It was impossible to be bored in my father's company. He was too sparky a man for that. Plots and plans and new ideas came flying off him like sparks from a grindstone.

"There's a good wind today," he said one Saturday morning. "Just right for flying a kite. Let's make a kite, Danny."

So we made a kite. He showed me how to splice four thin sticks together in the shape of a star, with two more sticks across the middle to brace it. Then we cut up an old blue shirt of his and stretched the material across the framework of the kite. We added a long tail made of thread, with little leftover pieces of the shirt tied at intervals along it. We found a ball of string in the workshop, and he showed me how to attach the string to the framework so that the kite would be properly balanced in flight.

Together we walked to the top of the hill behind the filling station to release the kite. I found it hard to believe that this object, made only from a few sticks and a piece of old shirt, would actually fly. I held the string while my father held the kite, and the moment he let it go, it caught the wind and soared upward like a huge blue bird.

"Let out some more, Danny!" he cried. "Go on! As much as you like!"

Higher and higher soared the kite. Soon it was just a small blue dot dancing in the sky miles above my head, and it was thrilling to stand there holding on to something that was so far away and so very much alive. This faraway thing was tugging and struggling on the end of the line like a big fish.

"Let's walk it back to the caravan," my father said.

So we walked down the hill again with me holding the string and the kite still pulling fiercely on the other end.

When we came to the caravan we were careful not to get the string tangled in the apple tree and we brought it all the way around to the front steps.

"Tie it to the steps," my father said.

"Will it still stay up?" I asked.

"It will if the wind doesn't drop," he said.

The wind didn't drop. And I will tell you something amazing. That kite stayed up there all through the night, and at breakfast time next morning the small blue dot was still dancing and swooping in the sky. After breakfast I hauled it down and hung it carefully against a wall in the workshop for another day.

Not long after that, on a lovely still evening when there was no breath of wind anywhere, my father said to me, "This is just the right weather for a fire balloon. Let's make a fire balloon."

He must have planned this one beforehand because he had

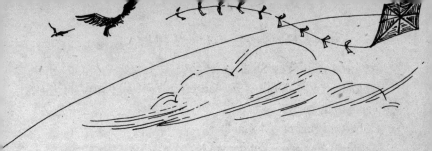

already bought the four big sheets of tissue paper and the pot of glue from Mr. Witton's bookshop in the village. And now, using only paper, glue, a pair of scissors, and a piece of thin wire, he made me a huge magnificent fire balloon in less than fifteen minutes. In the opening at the bottom, he tied a ball of cotton, and we were ready to go.

It was getting dark when we carried it outside into the field behind the caravan. We had with us a bottle of Sterno and some matches. I held the balloon upright while my father crouched underneath it and carefully poured a little Sterno onto the ball of cotton.

"Here goes," he said, putting a match to the cotton. "Hold the sides out as much as you can, Danny!"

A tall yellow flame leaped up from the ball of cotton and went right inside the balloon.

"It'll catch on fire!" I cried.

"No it won't," he said. "Watch!"

Between us, we held the sides of the balloon out as much as possible to keep them away from the flame in the early stages. But soon the hot air filled the balloon and the danger was over.

"She's nearly ready!" my father said. "Can you feel her floating?"

"Yes!" I said. "Yes! Shall we let go?"

"Not yet! . . . Wait a bit longer! . . . Wait until she's tugging to fly away!"

"She's tugging now!" I said.

"Right!" he cried. "Let her go!"

Slowly, majestically, and in absolute silence, our wonderful balloon began to rise up into the night sky.

"It flies!" I shouted, clapping my hands and jumping about. "It flies! It flies!"

My father was nearly as excited as I was. "It's a beauty," he said. "This one's a real beauty. You never know how they're going to turn out until you fly them. Each one is different."

Up and up it went, rising very fast now in the cool night air. It was like a magic fireball in the sky.

"Will other people see it?" I asked.

"I'm sure they will, Danny. It's high enough now for them to see it for miles around."

"What will they think it is, dad?"

"A flying saucer," my father said. "They'll probably call the police."

A small breeze had taken hold of the balloon and was carrying it away in the direction of the village.

"Let's follow it," my father said. "And with luck we'll find it when it comes down."

We ran to the road. We ran along the road. We kept running.

"She's coming down!" my father shouted. "The flame's

nearly gone out!"

We lost sight of it when the flame went out, but we guessed roughly which field it would be landing in, and we climbed over a gate and ran toward the place. For half an hour we searched the field in the darkness, but we couldn't find our balloon.

The next morning I went back alone to search again. I searched four big fields before I found it. It was lying in the corner of a field that was full of black and white cows. The cows were all standing around it and staring at it with their huge wet eyes. But they hadn't harmed it one bit. So I carried it home and hung it up alongside the kite, against a wall in the workshop, for another day.

"You can fly the kite all by yourself any time you like," my father said. "But you must never fly the fire balloon unless I'm with you. It is extremely dangerous."

"All right," I said.

"Promise me."

"I promise."

Then there was the treehouse which we built high up in the top of the big oak at the bottom of our meadow.

And the bow and arrow, the bow a four-foot-long ash sapling, and the arrows flighted with the tail feathers of partridge and pheasant.

And stilts that made me ten feet tall.

And a boomerang that came back and fell at my feet nearly every time I threw it.

And for my last birthday, there had been something that was more fun, perhaps, than anything else. The two days before by birthday, I'd been forbidden to enter the workshop because my father was in there working on a secret. And on the birthday morning, out came an amazing machine made from four bicycle wheels and several large soapboxes. But this was no ordinary whizzer. It had a brake pedal, a steering wheel, a comfortable seat, and a strong front bumper to take the shock of a crash. I called it "Soapo" and just about every day I would take it up to the top of the hill in the field behind the filling station and come shooting down again at incredible speeds, riding it like a bronco over the bumps.

So you can see that being eight years old and living with my father was a lot of fun. But I was impatient to be nine. I reckoned that being nine would be even more fun than being eight.

As it turned out, I was not altogether right about this.

My ninth year was certainly more *exciting* than any of the others. But not all of it was exactly what you would call fun.

4

My Father's Deep Dark Secret

HERE I AM AT the age of nine. This picture was made just before all the excitement started and I didn't have a worry in the world.

You will learn as you get older, just as I learned that autumn, that no father is perfect. Grown-ups are complicated creatures, full of quirks and secrets. Some have quirkier quirks and deeper secrets than others, but all of them, including one's own parents, have two or three private habits hidden up their sleeves that would probably make you gasp if you knew about them.

The rest of this book is about a most private and secret habit my father had, and about the strange adventures it led us both into.

It all started on a Saturday evening. It was the first Saturday of September. Around six o'clock my father and I had supper together in the caravan as usual. Then I went to bed. My father told me a fine story and kissed me good night. I fell asleep.

For some reason, I woke up again during the night. I lay still, listening for the sound of my father's breathing in the bunk above mine. I could hear nothing. He wasn't there, I was certain of that. This meant he had gone back to the workshop to finish a job. He often did that after he had tucked me in.

I listened for the usual workshop sounds—the little clinking noises of metal against metal or the tap of a hammer. They always comforted me tremendously, those noises in the night, because they told me my father was close at hand.

But on this night, no sound came from the workshop. The filling station was silent.

I got out of my bunk and found a box of matches by the sink. I struck one and held it up to the funny old clock that hung on the wall above the kettle. It said ten past eleven.

I went to the door of the caravan. "Dad," I said softly. "Dad, are you there?"

No answer.

There was a small wooden platform outside the caravan door, about four feet above the ground. I stood on the platform and gazed around me. "Dad!" I called out. "Where are you?"

Still no answer.

In pajamas and bare feet, I went down the caravan steps and crossed over to the workshop. I switched on the light. The old car we had been working on through the day was still there, but not my father.

I have already told you he did not have a car of his own, so there was no question of him having gone for a drive. He wouldn't have done that anyway. I was sure he would never willingly have left me alone in the filling station at night.

In which case, I thought, he must have fainted suddenly from some awful illness or fallen down and banged his head.

I would need a light if I was going to find him. I took the flashlight from the bench in the workshop.

I looked in the office. I went around and searched behind the office and behind the workshop.

I ran down the field to the lavatory. It was empty.

"Dad!" I shouted into the darkness. "Dad! Where are you?"

I ran back to the caravan. I shone the light into his bunk to make absolutely sure he wasn't there.

He wasn't in his bunk.

I stood in the dark caravan and for the first time in my life I felt a touch of panic. The filling station was a long way from the nearest farmhouse. I took the blanket from my bunk and put it around my shoulders. Then I went out the caravan door and sat on the platform with my feet on the top step of the ladder. There was a new moon in the sky, and across the road the big meadow lay pale and deserted in the moonlight. The silence was deathly.

I don't know how long I sat there. It may have been one hour. It could have been two. But I never dozed off. I wanted to keep listening all the time. If I listened very carefully I might hear something that would tell me where he was.

Then, at last, from far away, I heard the faint tap-tap of footsteps on the road.

The footsteps were coming closer and closer.

Tap . . . tap . . . tap . . . tap . . .

Was it him? Or was it somebody else?

I sat still, watching the road. I couldn't see very far along it. It faded away into a misty moonlit darkness.

Tap . . . tap . . . tap . . . tap . . . came the footsteps.

Then out of the mist a figure appeared.

It was him!

I jumped down the steps and ran onto the road to meet him.

"Danny!" he cried. "What on earth's the matter?"

"I thought something awful had happened to you," I said.

He took my hand in his and walked me back to the caravan in silence. Then he tucked me into my bunk. "I'm so sorry," he said. "I should never have done it. But you don't usually wake up, do you?"

"Where did you go, dad?"

"You must be tired out," he said.

"I'm not a bit tired. Couldn't we light the lamp for a little while?"

My father put a match to the wick of the lamp hanging from the ceiling, and the little yellow flame sprang up and filled the inside of the caravan with pale light. "How about a hot drink?" he said.

"Yes, please."

He lit the kerosene burner and put the kettle on to boil.

"I have decided something," he said. "I am going to let you in on the deepest, darkest secret of my whole life."

I was sitting up in my bunk watching my father.

"You asked me where I had been," he said. "The truth is I was up in Hazell's Wood."

"Hazell's Wood!" I cried. "That's miles away!"

"Six miles and a half," my father said. "I know I shouldn't have gone and I'm very, very sorry about it, but I had such a powerful yearning . . ." His voice trailed away into nothingness.

"But why would you want to go all the way up to Hazell's Wood?" I asked.

He spooned cocoa powder and sugar into two mugs, doing it very slowly and leveling each spoonful as though he were measuring medicine.

"Do you know what is meant by poaching?" he asked.

"Poaching? Not really, no."

"It means going up into the woods in the dead of night and coming back with something for the pot. Poachers in other places poach all sorts of different things, but around here it's always pheasants."

"You mean *stealing* them?" I said, aghast.

"We don't look at it that way," my father said. "Poaching is an art. A great poacher is a great artist."

"Is that actually what you were doing in Hazell's Wood, dad? Poaching pheasants?"

"I was practicing the art," he said. "The art of poaching."

I was shocked. My own father a thief! This gentle, lovely man! I couldn't believe he would go creeping into the woods at night to pinch valuable birds belonging to somebody else. "The kettle's boiling," I said.

"Ah, so it is." He poured the water into the mugs and brought mine over to me. Then he fetched his own and sat with it at the end of my bunk.

"Your grandad," he said, "my own dad, was a magnificent and splendiferous poacher. It was he who taught me all about it. I caught the poaching fever from him when I was ten years old and I've never lost it since. Mind you, in those days, just about every man in our village was out in the woods at night poaching pheasants. And they did it not only because they loved the sport but because they needed food for their families. When I was a boy, times were bad for a lot of people in England. There was very little work to be had anywhere, and some families were literally starving. Yet a few miles away in the rich man's wood, thousands of pheasants were being fed like kings twice a day. So can you blame my dad for going out occasionally and coming home with a bird or two for the family to eat?"

"No," I said. "Of course not. But we're not starving here, dad."

"You've missed the point, Danny boy! You've missed the whole point! Poaching is such a fabulous and exciting sport that once you start doing it, it gets into your blood and you can't give it up. Just imagine," he said, leaping off the bunk and waving his mug in the air, "just imagine for a minute that you are all alone up there in the dark wood, and the wood is full of keepers hiding behind the trees and the keepers have guns—"

"Guns!" I gasped. "They don't have guns!"

"All keepers have guns, Danny. It's for the vermin mostly, the foxes and stoats and weasels who go after the pheasants. But they'll always take a pot at a poacher, too, if they spot him."

"Dad, you're joking."

"Not at all. But they only do it from behind. Only when you're trying to escape. They like to pepper you in the legs at about fifty yards."

"They can't do that!" I cried. "They could go to prison for shooting someone!"

"You could go to prison for poaching," my father said. There was a glint and a sparkle in his eyes now that I had never seen before. "Many's the night when I was a boy, Danny, I've gone into the kitchen and seen my old dad lying face downward on the table and mum standing over him digging the gunshot pellets out of his backside with a potato knife."

"It's not true," I said, starting to laugh.

"You don't believe me?"

"Yes, I believe you."

"Toward the end, he was so covered in tiny little white scars he looked exactly like it was snowing."

"I don't know why I'm laughing," I said. "It's not funny, it's horrible."

"Poacher's bottom, they used to call it," my father said. "And there wasn't a man in the whole village who didn't have a bit of it one way or another. But my dad was the champion. How's the cocoa?"

"Fine, thank you."

"If you're hungry, we could have a midnight feast," he said.

"Could we, dad?"

"Of course."

My father got out the breadbox and the butter and cheese and started making sandwiches.

"Let me tell you about this phony pheasant-shooting business," he said. "First of all, it is practiced only by the rich. Only the very rich can afford to rear pheasants just for the fun of shooting them down when they grow up. These wealthy idiots spend huge sums of money every year buying baby pheasants from pheasant farms and rearing them in pens until they are big enough to be put out into the woods. In the woods, the young birds hang around like flocks of chickens. They are guarded by keepers and fed twice a day on the best corn until they're so fat they can hardly fly. Then beaters are hired who walk through the woods clapping their hands and making as much noise as they can to drive the half-tame pheasants toward the half-baked men and their guns. After that, it's *bang, bang, bang,* and down they come. Would you like strawberry jam on one of these?"

"Yes, please," I said. "One jam and one cheese. But, dad—"

"What?"

"How do you actually catch the pheasants when you're poaching? Do you have a gun hidden away up there?"

"A gun!" he cried, disgusted. "Real poachers don't *shoot* pheasants, Danny, didn't you know that? You've only got to fire a *cap pistol* up in those woods and the keepers'll be on you."

"Then how do you do it?"

"Ah," my father said, and the eyelids drooped over the eyes, veiled and secretive. He spread strawberry jam thickly on a piece of bread, taking his time.

"These things are big secrets," he said. "Very big secrets indeed. But I reckon if my father could tell them to me, then maybe I can tell them to you. Would you like me to do that?"

"Yes," I said. "Tell me now."

5
❧

The Secret Methods

"ALL THE BEST WAYS of poaching pheasants were discovered by my old dad," my father said. "My old dad studied poaching the way a scientist studies science."

My father put my sandwiches on a plate and brought them over to my bunk. I put the plate on my lap and started eating. I was ravenous.

"Do you know, my old dad actually used to keep a flock of prime roosters in the back yard just to practice on," my father said. "A rooster is very much like a pheasant, you see. They are equally stupid and they like the same sort of foods. A rooster is tamer, that's all. So whenever my dad thought up a new method of catching pheasants, he tried it out on a rooster first to see if it worked."

"What are the best ways?" I asked.

My father laid a half-eaten sandwich on the edge of the sink and gazed at me in silence for about twenty seconds. "Promise you won't tell another soul?"

"I promise."

"Now here's the thing," he said. "Here's the first big

secret. Ah, but it's more than a secret, Danny. It's the most important discovery in the whole history of poaching."

He edged a shade closer to me. His face was pale in the pale yellow glow from the lamp in the ceiling, but his eyes were shining like stars.

"So here it is," he said, and now suddenly his voice became soft and whispery and very private. "*Pheasants*," he whispered, "*are crazy about raisins.*"

"Is that the big secret?"

"That's it," he said. "It may not sound very much when I say it like that, but believe me it is."

"Raisins?" I said.

"Just ordinary raisins. It's like a *mania* with them. You throw a few raisins into a bunch of pheasants and they'll start fighting each other to get at them. My dad discovered that forty years ago, just as he discovered these other things I am about to describe to you."

My father paused and glanced over his shoulder as though to make sure there was nobody at the door of the caravan, listening. "Method Number One," he said softly, "is known as *The Horsehair Stopper*."

"*The Horsehair Stopper*," I murmured.

"That's it," my father said. "And the reason it's such a brilliant method is that it's completely silent. There's no squawking or flapping around or anything else with *The Horsehair Stopper* when the pheasant is caught. And that's mighty important because don't forget, Danny, when you're up in those woods at night and the great trees are spreading their branches high above you like black ghosts, it is so silent you can hear a mouse moving. And somewhere among it all, the keepers are waiting and listening. They're always there, those keepers, standing stony still against a tree or behind a bush with their guns at the ready."

"What happens with *The Horsehair Stopper?*" I asked. "How does it work?"

"It's very simple," he said. "First, you take a few raisins and you soak them in water overnight to make them plump and soft and juicy. Then you get a bit of good stiff horsehair and you cut it up into half-inch lengths."

"Horsehair?" I said. "Where do you get horsehair?"

"You pull it out of a horse's tail, of course. That's not difficult as long as you stand to one side when you're doing it so you don't get kicked."

"Go on," I said.

"So you cut the horsehair up into half-inch lengths. Then you push one of these lengths through the middle of a raisin so there's just a tiny bit of horsehair sticking out on each side. That's all you do. You are now ready to catch a pheasant. If you want to catch more than one, you prepare more raisins. Then, when evening comes, you creep up into the woods, making sure you get there before the pheasants have gone up into the trees to roost. Then you scatter the raisins. And soon, along comes a pheasant and gobbles one up."

"What happens then?" I asked.

"Here's what my dad discovered," he said. "First of all, the horsehair makes the raisin stick in the pheasant's throat. It

doesn't hurt him. It simply stays there and tickles. It's rather like having a crumb stuck in your own throat. But after that, believe it or not, the *pheasant never moves his feet again!* He becomes absolutely rooted to the spot, and there he stands pumping his silly neck up and down just like a piston, and all you've got to do is nip out quickly from the place where you're hiding and pick him up."

"Is that really true, dad?"

"I swear it," my father said. "Once a pheasant's had *The Horsehair Stopper,* you can turn a hosepipe on him and he won't move. It's just one of those unexplainable little things. But it takes a genius to discover it."

My father paused, and there was a gleam of pride in his eyes as he dwelt for a moment upon the memory of his own dad, the great poaching inventor.

"So that's Method Number One," he said.

"What's Number Two?" I asked.

"Ah," he said. "Number Two's a real beauty. It's a flash of pure brilliance. I can even remember that day it was invented. I was just about the same age you are now, and it was a Sunday morning, and my dad comes into the kitchen holding a huge white rooster in his hands. 'I think I've got it,' he says. There's a little smile on his face and a shine of glory in his eyes and he comes in very soft and quick and puts the bird down right in the middle of the kitchen table. 'By golly,' he says, 'I've got a good one this time.'

" 'A good what?' mum says, looking up from the sink. 'Horace, take that filthy bird off my table.'

"The rooster has a funny little paper hat over its head, like an ice-cream cone upside down, and my dad is pointing to it proudly and saying, 'Stroke him. Go on, stroke him. Do anything you like to him. He won't move an inch.' The rooster starts scratching away at the paper hat with one of its feet, but the hat seems to be stuck on and won't come off. 'No bird in the world is going to run away once you cover up its eyes,' my dad says, and he starts poking the rooster with his finger and pushing it around on the table. The rooster doesn't take the slightest bit of notice. 'You can have this one,' he says to mum. 'You can have it and ring its neck and dish it up for dinner as a celebration of what I have just invented.'

"And then straightaway he takes me by the arm and marches me quickly out the door and off we go over the fields and up into the big forest the other side of Little Hampden which used to belong to the Duke of Buckingham. And in less than two hours we get five lovely fat pheasants with no more trouble than it takes to go out and buy them in a shop."

My father paused for breath. His eyes were shining bright as they gazed back into the wonderful world of his youth.

"But, dad," I said. "How do you get the paper hats over the pheasants' heads?"

"You'd never guess it, Danny."

"Tell me."

"Listen carefully," he said, glancing again over his shoulder as though he expected to see a keeper or even the Duke of Buckingham himself at the caravan door. "Here's how you do it. First of all, you dig a little hole in the ground. Then you twist a piece of paper into the shape of a cone and you fit this into the hole, hollow end up, like a cup. Then you smear the inside of the paper cup with glue and drop in a few raisins. At the same time, you lay a trail of raisins along the ground leading up to it. Now, the old pheasant comes pecking along the trail, and when he gets to the hole he pops his head inside to gobble up the raisins and the next thing he knows he's got a paper hat stuck over his eyes and he can't see a thing. Isn't that a fantastic idea, Danny? My dad called it *The Sticky Hat*."

"Is that the one you used this evening?" I asked.

My father nodded.

"How many did you get, dad?"

"Well," he said, looking a bit sheepish. "Actually I didn't get any. I arrived too late. By the time I got there they were already going up to roost. That shows you how out of practice I am."

"Was it fun all the same?"

"Marvelous," he said. "Absolutely marvelous. Just like the old days."

He undressed and put on his pajamas. Then he turned out the lamp in the ceiling and climbed up into his bunk.

"Dad," I whispered.

"What is it?"

"Have you been doing this often after I've gone to sleep, without me knowing it?"

"No," he said. "Tonight was the first time for nine years. When your mother died and I had to look after you by myself, I made a vow to give up poaching until you were old enough to be left alone at nights. But this evening I broke my vow. I had such a tremendous longing to go up into the woods again, I just couldn't stop myself. I'm very sorry I did it."

"If you ever want to go again, I won't mind," I said.

"Do you mean that?" he said, his voice rising in excitement. "Do you really mean it?"

"Yes," I said. "So long as you tell me beforehand. You will promise to tell me beforehand if you're going, won't you?"

"You're quite sure you won't mind?"

"Quite sure."

"Good boy," he said. "And we'll have roast pheasant for supper whenever you want it. It's miles better than chicken."

"And one day, dad, will you take me with you?"

"Ah," he said, "I reckon you're just a bit young to be dodging around up there in the dark. I wouldn't want you to get peppered with buckshot in the backside at your age."

"Your dad took you at my age," I said.

There was a short silence.

"We'll see how it goes," my father said. "But I'd like to get back into practice before I make any promises, you understand?"

"Yes," I said.

"I wouldn't want to take you with me until I'm right back in my old form."

"No," I said.

"Good night, Danny. Go to sleep now."

"Good night, dad."

6

❧

Mr. Victor Hazell

THE FOLLOWING FRIDAY, while we were having supper in the caravan, my father said, "If it's all right with you, Danny, I'll be going out again tomorrow night."

"You mean poaching?"

"Yes."

"Will it be Hazell's Wood again?"

"It'll always be Hazell's Wood," he said. "First, because that's where all the pheasants are. And second, because I don't like Mr. Hazell one little bit, and it's a pleasure to poach his birds."

I must pause here to tell you something about Mr. Victor Hazell. He was a brewer of beer and he owned a huge brewery. He was rich beyond words, and his property stretched for miles along either side of the valley. All the land around us belonged to him, everything on either side of the road, everything except the small patch of ground on which our filling station stood. That patch belonged to my father. It was a little island in the middle of the vast ocean of Mr. Hazell's estate.

Mr. Victor Hazell was a roaring snob and he tried desperately to get in with what he believed were the right kind of folk. He hunted with the hounds and gave shooting parties and wore fancy waistcoats. And every weekday he drove his enormous silver Rolls-Royce past our filling station on his way to the brewery. As he flashed by we would sometimes catch a glimpse of the great, glistening beery face above the wheel, pink as a ham, all soft and inflamed from drinking too much beer.

"No," my father said, "I do not like Mr. Victor Hazell one little bit. I haven't forgotten the way he spoke to you last year when he came in for a fill-up."

I hadn't forgotten it either. Mr. Hazell had pulled up alongside the pumps in his glistening, gleaming Rolls-Royce and had said to me, "Fill her up and look sharp about it." I was eight years old at the time. He didn't get out of the car, he just handed me the key to the cap of the gasoline tank and as he did so, he barked out, "And keep your filthy little hands to yourself, you understand?"

I didn't understand at all, so I said, "What do you mean, sir?"

There was a leather riding crop on the seat beside him. He picked it up and pointed it at me like a pistol. "If you make any dirty fingermarks on my paintwork," he said, "I'll step right out of this car and give you a good hiding."

My father was out of the workshop almost before Mr. Hazell had finished speaking. He strode up to the window of the car and placed his hands on the sill and leaned in. "I don't like you speaking to my son like that," he said. His voice was dangerously soft.

Mr. Hazell did not look at him. He sat quite still in the seat of his Rolls-Royce, his tiny piggy eyes staring straight ahead. There was a smug superior little smile around the corners of his mouth.

"You had no reason to threaten him," my father went on. "He had done nothing wrong."

Mr. Hazell continued to act as though my father wasn't there.

"Next time you threaten someone with a good hiding I suggest you pick on a person your own size," my father said. "Like me, for instance."

Mr. Hazell still did not move.

"Now go away, please," my father said. "We do not wish to serve you." He took the key from my hand and tossed it through the window. The Rolls-Royce drove away fast in a cloud of dust.

The very next day, an inspector from the local Department of Health arrived and said he had come to inspect our caravan.

"What do you want to inspect our caravan for?" my father asked.

"To see if it's a fit place for humans to live in," the man said. "We don't allow people to live in dirty broken-down shacks these days."

My father showed him the inside of the caravan which was spotlessly clean as always and as cozy as could be, and in the end the man had to admit there was nothing wrong with it.

Soon after that, another inspector turned up and took a sample of gasoline from one of our underground storage tanks. My father explained to me they were checking up to see if we were mixing some of our second-grade gasoline in with the first-grade stuff, which is an old dodge practiced by crooked filling station owners. Of course we were not doing this.

Hardly a week went by without some local official dropping by to check up on one thing or another, and there was little doubt, my father said, that the long and powerful arm of Mr. Hazell was reaching out behind the scenes and trying to run us off our land.

So, all in all, you can see why it gave my father a certain pleasure to poach Mr. Victor Hazell's pheasants.

That night, we put the raisins in to soak.

The next day was poaching day, and don't think my father didn't know it. From the moment he got out of his bunk in the morning the excitement began to build up inside him. This was a Saturday so I was home from school, and we spent most of the day in the workshop decarbonizing the cylinders of Mr. Pratchett's Austin Seven. It was a great little car, built in 1933, a tiny miracle of a machine that still ran as sweetly as ever though it was now more than forty years old. My father said that these Austin Sevens, better known in their time as Baby Austins, were the first successful mini-cars ever made. Mr. Pratchett, who owned a turkey farm near Aylesbury, was as proud as could be of this one, and he always brought it to us for repair.

Working together, we released the valve springs and drew out the valves. We unscrewed the cylinder head nuts and lifted off the head itself. Then we began scraping the carbon from the inside of the head and from the top of the pistons.

"I want to be away by six o'clock," my father said. "Then I will get to the wood exactly at twilight."

"Why at twilight?" I asked.

"Because at twilight everything inside the wood becomes veiled and shady. You can see to move around but it's not easy for someone else to see you. And when danger threatens you can always hide in the shadows which are darker than a wolf's mouth."

"Why don't you wait till it gets really dark?" I asked. "Then you wouldn't be seen at all."

"You wouldn't catch anything if you did that," he said. "When night comes on, all the pheasants fly up into the trees to roost. Pheasants are just like other birds. They never sleep on the ground. Twilight," my father added, "begins around seven thirty this week. And as it's at least an hour and a half's walk to the wood, I must not leave here later than six o'clock."

"Are you going to use *The Sticky Hat* or will it be *The Horsehair Stopper*?" I asked.

"*Sticky Hat*," he said. "I'm very fond of *Sticky Hat*."

"When will you be back?"

"About ten o'clock," he said. "Ten thirty at the latest. I promise I'll be back by ten thirty. You're quite sure you don't mind being left alone?"

"Quite sure," I said. "But you will be all right, won't you, dad?"

"Don't you worry about me," he said, putting his arm around my shoulders and giving me a hug.

"But you said there wasn't a man in your dad's village that didn't get a bit shot up by the keepers sooner or later."

"Ah," my father said. "Yes. I did say that, didn't I? But in those days there were lots more keepers up in the woods than there are now. There were keepers behind almost every tree."

"How many are there now in Hazell's Wood?"

"Not too many," he said. "Not too many at all."

As the day wore on, I could see my father getting more and more impatient and excited. By five o'clock we had finished work on the Baby Austin, and together we ran her up and down the road to test her out.

At five thirty we had an early supper of sausages and bacon, but my father hardly ate anything at all.

At six o'clock precisely, he kissed me good-bye and said, "Promise not to wait up for me, Danny. Put yourself to bed at eight and go to sleep. Right?"

He set off down the road and I stood on the platform of the caravan, watching him go. I loved the way he moved. He had that long, loping stride all countrymen have who are used to covering great distances on foot. He was wearing an old navy-blue sweater and an even older cap on his head. He turned and waved to me. I waved back. Then he disappeared around a bend in the road.

7

❧

The Baby Austin

INSIDE THE CARAVAN I stood on a chair and lit the oil lamp in the ceiling. I had some weekend homework to do, and this was as good a time as any to do it. I laid my books out on the table and sat down. But I found it impossible to keep my mind on my work.

The clock said half past seven. This was the twilight time. He would be there now. I pictured him in his old navy-blue sweater and peaked cap walking soft-footed up the track toward the wood. He told me he wore the sweater because navy blue hardly showed up at all in the dark. Black was even better, he said. But he didn't have a black sweater and navy blue was next best. The peaked cap was important too, he explained, because the peak cast a shadow over one's face. Just about now he would be wriggling through the hedge and entering the wood. Inside the wood I could see him treading carefully over the leafy ground, stopping, listening, going on again, and all the time searching and searching for the keeper who would somewhere be standing still as a post beside a big tree, a gun under his arm. Keepers hardly move at all when they are in a wood watching for poachers, he had told me. They stand dead still right up against the trunk of a tree, and it's not easy to spot a motionless man in that position at twilight when the shadows are as dark as a wolf's mouth.

I closed my books. It was no good trying to work. I decided to go to bed instead. I undressed and put on my pajamas and climbed into my bunk. I left the lamp burning. Soon, I fell asleep.

When I opened my eyes again, the oil lamp was still glowing and the clock on the wall said ten minutes past two.

Ten minutes past two!

I jumped out of my bunk and looked into the bunk above mine. It was empty.

He had promised he would be home by ten thirty at the latest, and he never broke promises.

He was nearly four hours overdue!

At that moment, a frightful sense of doom came over me. Something really had happened to him this time. I felt quite certain of it.

Hold it, I told myself. Don't get panicky. Last week you got all panicky and you made a bit of a fool of yourself.

Yes, but last week was a different thing altogether. He had made no promises to me last week. This time he had said, "I promise I'll be back by ten thirty." Those were his exact words. And he never, absolutely never, broke a promise.

I looked again at the clock. He had left the caravan at six, which meant *he had been gone over eight hours!*

It took me two seconds to decide what I should do.

Very quickly I stripped off my pajamas and put on my shirt and my jeans. Perhaps the keepers had shot him up so badly he couldn't walk. I slipped my sweater over my head. It was neither navy blue nor black. It was a sort of pale brown. It would have to do. Perhaps he was lying in the wood bleeding to death. My sneakers were the wrong color, too. They were white. But they were also dirty and that took a lot of the whiteness away. How long would it take me to get to the wood? One hour and a half. Less if I ran most of the way, but not much less. As I bent down to tie the laces, I noticed my hands were shaking. And my stomach had that awful prickly feeling as though it were full of small needles.

I ran down the steps of the caravan and across to the workshop to get the flashlight. A flashlight is a good companion when you are alone outdoors at night, and I wanted it with me. I grabbed the flashlight and went out of the workshop. I paused for a moment beside the pumps. The moon had long since disappeared, but the sky was clear, and a great mass of stars was wheeling above my head. There was no wind at all, no sound of any kind. To my right, going away into the blackness of the countryside, lay the lonely road that led to the dangerous wood.

Six and a half miles.

Thank heaven I knew the way.

But it was going to be a long, hard slog. I must try to keep a good steady pace and not run myself to a standstill in the first mile.

At that point a wild and marvelous idea came to me.

Why shouldn't I go in the Baby Austin? I really did know how to drive. My father had always allowed me to move the automobiles around when they came in for repair. He let me drive them into the workshop and back them out again afterward. And sometimes I drove one of them slowly around the pumps in first gear. I loved doing it. And I would get there much much quicker if I went by car. This was an emergency. If he was wounded and bleeding badly, then every minute counted. I had never driven on the road, but I would surely not meet any other cars at this time of night. I would go very slowly and keep close in to the hedge on the proper side.

I went back to the workshop and switched on the light. I opened the double doors. I got into the driver's seat of the Baby Austin. I turned on the ignition key. I pulled out the choke lever. I found the starter button on the floor near the gearbox and pressed it. The motor coughed once, then started.

Now for the lights. There was a pointed switch on the dashboard and I turned it to S for sidelights only. The sidelights came on. I felt for the clutch pedal with my toe. I was just able to reach it, but I had to point my toe if I wanted to press it all the way down. I pressed it down. Then I slipped the gear lever into reverse. Slowly I backed the car out of the workshop.

I left her ticking over and went back to switch off the workshop light. It was better to keep everything looking as normal as possible. The filling station was in darkness now except for a dim light coming from the caravan where the little oil lamp was still burning. I decided to leave that on.

I got back into the car. I closed the door. The sidelights were so dim I hardly knew they were there. I switched on the headlights. That was better. I searched for the dimmer with my foot. I found it. I tried it and it worked. I put the headlights on full. If I met another car, I must remember to dim them, although actually they weren't bright enough to dazzle a cockroach. They didn't give any more light than a couple of good flashlights.

I pressed down the clutch pedal again and pushed the gear lever into first. This was it. My heart was thumping away so fiercely I could hear it in my throat. Ten yards away lay the public highway. It was as dark as doomsday. I released the clutch very slowly. At the same time, I pressed down just a fraction of an inch on the accelerator, and stealthily, oh, most wonderfully, the little car began to lean forward and steal into motion. I pressed a shade harder on the accelerator. We crept out of the filling station onto the dark, deserted road.

I will not pretend I wasn't petrified. I was. But mixed in with the awful fear was a glorious feeling of excitement. Most of the really exciting things we do in our lives scare us to death. They wouldn't be exciting if they didn't. I sat very stiff and upright in my seat, gripping the steering wheel tight with both hands. My eyes were about level with the top of the steering wheel. I could have done with a cushion to raise me up higher, but it was too late for that.

The road seemed awfully narrow in the dark. I knew there was room enough for two cars to pass each other. I had seen them from the filling station doing it a million times. But it didn't look that way to me from where I was. At any moment, something with blazing headlights might come roaring toward me at sixty miles an hour, a giant truck or one of those big long-distance buses that travel through the night full of passengers. Was I too much in the middle of the road? Yes, I was. But I didn't want to pull in closer for fear of hitting the bank. If I hit the bank and busted the front axle, then all would be lost and I would never get my father home.

The motor was beginning to rattle and shake. I was still in first gear. It was vital I change up into second, otherwise the engine would get too hot. I knew how the change was done but I had never actually tried doing it. Around the filling station I had always stayed in first gear.

Well, here goes.

I eased my foot off the accelerator. I pressed down the clutch and held it there. I found the gear lever and pulled it straight back, from first into second. I released the clutch and pressed on the accelerator. The little car leaped forward as though it had been stung. We were in second gear.

What speed were we going? I glanced at the speedometer. It was lit up very faintly, but I was able to read it. It said fifteen miles an hour. Good. That was quite fast enough. I would stay in second gear. I started figuring out how long it would take me to do six miles traveling at fifteen miles an hour.

At sixty miles an hour, six miles would take six minutes. At thirty, it would take twice as long, twelve minutes.

At fifteen, it would take twice as long again, twenty-four minutes.

I kept going. I knew every bit of the road, every curve and every little rise and dip. Once a fox flashed out of the hedge in front of me and ran across the road with his long bushy tail streaming out behind him. I saw him clearly in the glow of my headlights. His fur was red-brown and he had a white muzzle. It was a thrilling sight. I began to worry about the motor. I knew very well it would be certain to overheat if I drove for long in either first or second gear. I was in second. I must now change up into third. I took a deep breath and grasped the gear lever again. Foot off the accelerator. Clutch in. Gear lever up and across and up again. Clutch out. I had done it! I pressed down on the accelerator. The speedometer crept up to thirty. I gripped the wheel very tight with both hands and stayed in the middle of the road. At this rate, I would soon be there.

Hazell's Wood was not on the main road. To reach it you had to turn left through a gap in the hedge and go uphill over a bumpy track for about a quarter of a mile. If the ground had been wet, there would have been no hope of getting up there in a car. But there hadn't been any rain for a week and the ground would surely be hard and dry. I figured I must be getting pretty close to the turning place now. I must watch out for it carefully. It would be easy to miss it. There was no gate or anything else to indicate where it was. It was

simply a small gap in the hedge just wide enough to allow farm tractors to go through.

Suddenly, far ahead of me, just below the rim of the night sky, I saw a splash of yellow light. I watched it, trembling. This was something I had been dreading all along. Very quickly the light got brighter and brighter, and nearer and nearer, and in a few seconds it took shape and became the long white beam of headlights from an automobile rushing toward me.

My turning place must be very close now. I was desperate to reach it and swing off the road before that monster reached me. I pressed my foot hard down for more speed. The little engine roared. The speedometer needle went from thirty to thirty-five and then to forty. But the other car was closing fast. Its headlights were like two dazzling white eyes. They grew bigger and bigger and suddenly the whole road in front of me was lit up as clear as daylight, and *SWISH!* the thing went past me like a bullet. It was so close I felt the wind of it through my open window. And in that tiny fraction of a second when the two of us were alongside one another, I caught a glimpse of its white-painted body and I knew it was the police.

I didn't dare look around to see if they were stopping and coming back after me. I was certain they would stop. Any policeman in the world would stop if he suddenly passed a small boy in a tiny car chugging along a lonely road at half past two in the morning. My only thought was to get away, to escape, to vanish, though heaven knows how I was going to do that. I pressed my foot harder still on the accelerator. Then all at once I saw in my own dim headlights the tiny gap in the hedge on my left-hand side. There wasn't time to break or slow down, so I just yanked the wheel hard over and prayed. The little car swerved violently off the road, leaped through the gap, hit the rising ground, bounced high in the air, then skidded around sideways behind the hedge and stopped.

The first thing I did was to switch off all my lights. I am not quite sure what made me do this except that I knew I must hide and I knew that if you are hiding from someone in the dark, you do not shine lights all over the place to show where you are. I sat very still in my dark car. The hedge was a thick one and I couldn't see through it. The car had bounced and skidded sideways in such a way that it was now right off the track. It was behind the hedge and in a sort of field. It was facing back toward the filling station, tucked in very close to the hedge. I could hear the police car. It had pulled up about fifty yards down the road, and now it was backing and turning. The road was far too narrow for it to turn around in one go. Then the roar from the motor got louder and he came back fast with engine revving and headlights blazing. He flashed past the place where I was hiding and raced away into the night.

That meant the policeman had not seen me swing off the road.

But he was certain to come back again looking for me. And if he came back slowly enough, he would probably see the gap. He would stop and get out of his car. He would walk through the gap and look behind the hedge, and then . . . Then his flashlight would shine in my face and he would say, "What's going on, sonny? What's the big idea? Where do you think you're going? Whose car is this? Where do you live? Where are your parents?" He would make me come with him to the police station, and in the end they would get the whole story out of me, and my father would be ruined.

I sat quiet as a mouse and waited. I waited for a long time. Then I heard the sound of the motor coming back again in my direction. It was making a terrific noise. He was going flat out. He whizzed past me like a rocket. The way he was gunning that motor told me he was a very angry man. He must have been a very puzzled man, too. Perhaps he was thinking he had seen a ghost. A ghost boy driving a ghost car.

I waited to see if he was going to come back once again. He didn't come.

I switched on my lights.

I pressed the starter. She started at once.

But what about the wheels and the chassis? I felt sure something must have got broken when she jumped off the road onto the cart track.

I put her into gear and very gently began to ease her forward. I listened carefully for horrid noises. There were none. I managed to get her off the grass and back onto the track.

I drove very slowly now. The track was extremely rough and rutted, and the slope was pretty steep. The little car bounced and bumped all over the place, but she kept going. Then at last, ahead of me and over to the right, looking like some gigantic black creature crouching on the crest of the hill, I saw Hazell's Wood.

Soon I was there. Immense trees rose up toward the sky all along the right-hand side of the track. I stopped the car. I switched off the motor and the lights. I got out, taking the flashlight with me.

There was the usual hedge dividing the wood from the track. I squeezed my way through it and suddenly I was right inside the wood. When I looked up the trees had closed in above my head like a prison roof, and I couldn't see the smallest patch of sky or a single star. I couldnt' see anything at all. The darkness was so solid around me I could almost touch it.

"Dad!" I called out. "Dad, are you there?"

My small high voice echoed around the forest and faded away. I listened for an answer, but none came.

8

The Pit

I CANNOT POSSIBLY DESCRIBE to you what it felt like to be standing alone in the pitchy blackness of that silent wood in the small hours of the night. The sense of loneliness was overwhelming, the silence was as deep as death, and the only sounds were the ones I made myself. I tried to keep absolutely still for as long as possible, to see if I could hear anything at all. I listened and listened. I held my breath and listened again. I had a queer feeling that the whole wood was listening with me, the trees and the bushes, the little animals hiding in the undergrowth and the birds roosting in the branches. All were listening. Even the silence was listening.

I switched on the flashlight. A brilliant beam of light reached out ahead of me like a long white arm. That was better. Now at any rate I could see where I was going.

The keepers would also see. But I didn't care about the keepers any more. The only person I cared about was my father. I wanted him back.

I kept the flashlight on and went deeper into the wood.

"Dad!" I shouted. "Dad! It's Danny! Are you there?"

I didn't know which direction I was going in. I just went

on walking and calling out, walking and calling; and each time I called, I would stop and listen. But no answer came.

After a time, my voice began to go all trembly. I started to say silly things like, "Oh, dad, please tell me where you are! Please answer me! Please, oh, please. . . ." And I knew that if I wasn't careful, the sheer hopelessness of it all would get the better of me and I would simply give up and lie down under the trees.

"Are you there, dad? Are you there?" I shouted. "It's Danny!"

I stood still—listening, listening, listening. In the silence that followed, I heard, or thought I heard, the faint, but oh so faint, sound of a human voice.

I froze and kept listening.

Yes, there it was again.

I ran toward the sound. "Dad!" I shouted. "It's Danny! Where are you?"

I stopped again and listened.

This time the answer came loud enough for me to hear the words. "I'm here!" the voice called out. "Over here!"

It was him!

I was so excited my legs began to get all shaky.

"Where are you, Danny?" my father called out.

"I'm here, dad! I'm coming."

With the beam of the flashlight shining ahead of me, I ran toward the voice. The trees were bigger here and spaced farther apart. The ground was a carpet of brown leaves from last year and was good to run on. I didn't call out any more after that. I simply dashed ahead.

And all at once, his voice was right in front of me. "Stop, Danny, stop!" he shouted.

I stopped dead. I shone the flashlight over the ground. I couldn't see him.

"Where are you, dad?"

"I'm down here. Come forward slowly. But be careful. Don't fall in."

I crept forward. Then I saw the pit. I went to the edge of it and shone the light downward, and there was my father. He was sitting on the floor of the pit and he looked up into the light and said, "Hello, my marvelous darling. Thank you for coming."

"Are you all right, dad?"

"My ankle seems to be broken," he said. "It happened when I fell in."

The pit had been dug in the shape of a square, with each side about six feet long. But it was the depth of it that was so awful. It was at least twelve feet deep. The sides had been cut straight down into the earth, presumably with a mechanical shovel, and no man could have climbed out of it without help.

"Does it hurt?" I asked.

"Yes," he said. "It hurts a lot. But don't worry about that. The point is, *I've got to get out of here before morning.* The keepers know I'm here and they're coming back for me as soon as it gets light."

"Did they dig the hole to catch people?" I asked.

"Yes," he said.

I shone my light around the top of the pit and saw how the keepers had covered it over with sticks and leaves and how the whole thing had collapsed when my father stepped on it. It was the kind of trap hunters in Africa dig to catch wild animals.

"Do the keepers know who you are?" I asked.

"No," he said. "Two of them came and shone a light down on me but I covered my face in my arms and they couldn't recognize me. I heard them trying to guess. They were guessing all sorts of names but they didn't mention mine. Then one of them shouted, 'We'll find out who you are all right in the morning, my lad. And guess who's coming with us to fish you out?' I didn't answer. I didn't want them to hear my voice. 'We'll tell you who's coming,' the one said. 'Mr. Victor Hazell himself is coming with us to say hello to you!' And the other one said, 'Boy, I hate to think what he's going to do when he gets his hands on you!' They both laughed and then they went away. Ouch! My poor ankle!"

"Have the keepers gone, dad?"

"Yes," he said. "They've gone for the night."

I was kneeling on the edge of the pit. I wanted so badly to go down and comfort him, but that would have been madness.

"What time is it?" he said. "Shine the light down so I can see." I did as he asked. "It's ten to three," he said. "I must be out of here before sunrise."

"Dad," I said.

"Yes?"

"I brought the car. I came in the Baby Austin."

"You *what?*" he cried.

"I wanted to get here quickly so I just drove it out of the workshop and came straight here."

He sat there staring at me. I kept the flashlight pointed to one side of him so as not to dazzle his eyes.

"You mean you actually drove here in the Baby Austin?"

"Yes."

"You're crazy," he said. "You're absolutely plumb crazy."

"It wasn't difficult," I said.

"You could have got killed," he said. "If anything had hit you in that little thing, you'd have been smashed to smithereens."

"It went fine, dad."

"Where is it now?"

"Just outside the wood on the bumpy track."

His face was all puckered up with pain and as white as a sheet of paper.

"Are you all right?" I asked.

"Yes," he said. "I'm fine." He was shivering all over though it was a warm night.

"If we could get you out, I'm sure I could help you to the car," I said. "You could lean on me and hop on one leg."

"I'll never get out of here without a ladder," he said.

"Wouldn't a rope do?" I asked.

"A rope!" he said. "Yes, of course! A rope would do it. There's one in the Baby Austin. It's under the rear seat. Mr. Pratchett always carries a towrope in case of a breakdown."

"I'll get it," I said. "Wait there, dad."

I left him and ran back the way I had come, shining the flashlight ahead of me. I found the car. I lifted up the rear seat. The towrope was there, tangled up with the jack and the wheel brace. I got it out and slung it over my shoulder. I wriggled through the hedge and ran back into the wood.

"Where are you, dad?" I called out.

"Over here," he answered.

With his voice to guide me, I had no trouble finding him this time. "I've got the rope," I said.

"Good. Now, tie one end of it to the nearest tree."

Using the flashlight all the time, I tied one end of the rope around the nearest tree. I lowered the other end down to my father in the pit. He grasped it with both hands and hauled himself up into a standing position. He stood only on his right leg. He kept his left foot off the ground by bending his knee.

"Jeepers," he said. "This hurts."

"Do you think you can make it, dad?"

"I've got to make it," he said. "Is the rope tied properly?"

"Yes."

I lay on my stomach with my hands dangling down into the pit. I wanted to help pull him up as soon as he came within reach. I kept the flashlight on him all the time.

"I've got to climb this with hands only," he said.

"You can do it," I told him.

I saw his knuckles tighten as he gripped the rope. Then he came up, hand over hand, and as soon as he was within reach I got hold of one of his arms and pulled for all I was worth. He came over the top edge of the pit sliding on his chest and stomach, him pulling on the rope and me pulling on his arm. He lay on the ground, breathing fast and loud.

"You've done it!" I said.

"Let me rest a moment."

I waited, kneeling beside him.

"All right," he said. "Now for the next bit. Give me a hand, Danny. You'll have to do most of the work from now on."

I helped him to keep his balance as he got up onto his one good foot. "Which side do you want me on?" I asked.

"On my right," he said. "Otherwise you'll keep knocking against my bad ankle."

I moved up close to his right side, and he put both his hands on my shoulders.

"Go on, dad," I said. "You can lean harder than that."

"Shine the light forward so we can see where we're going," he said.

I did as he asked.

He tried a couple of hops on his right foot.

"All right?" I asked him.

"Yes," he said. "Let's go."

Holding his left foot just clear of the ground, and leaning on me with both hands, he began to hop forward on one leg. I shuffled along beside him, trying to go at exactly the speed he wanted.

"Say when you want a rest."

"Now," he said. We stopped. "I've got to sit down," he said. I helped him to lower himself to the ground. His left foot dangled helplessly on its broken ankle, and every time it touched the ground he jumped with pain. I sat beside him on the brown leaves that covered the floor of the wood. The sweat was pouring down his face.

"Does it hurt terribly, dad?"

"It does when I hop," he said. "Each time I hop, it jars it."

He sat on the ground resting for several minutes.

"Let's try again," he said.

I helped him up and off we went. This time I put one of my arms around his waist to give him extra support. He put his right arm around my shoulders and leaned on me hard. It went better that way. But boy, was he heavy. My legs kept bending and buckling with each hop.

Hop . . .

Hop . . .

Hop . . .

"Keep going," he gasped. "Come on. We can make it."

"There's the hedge," I said, waving the flashlight. "We're nearly there."

Hop . . .

Hop . . .

Hop . . .

When we reached the hedge, my legs gave way and we both crashed to the ground.

"I'm sorry," I said.

"It's O.K. Can you help me get through the hedge?"

I'm not quite sure how he and I got through that hedge. He crawled a bit and I pulled a bit, and little by little we squeezed through and out the other side onto the track. The tiny car was only ten yards away.

We sat on the grassy bank under the hedge to get a breather. His watch said it was nearly four o'clock in the morning. The sun would not be up for another two hours, so we had plenty of time.

"Shall I drive?" I asked.

"You'll have to," he said. "I've only got one foot."

I helped him to hop over to the car, and after a bit of a struggle he managed to get in. His left leg was doubled up underneath his right leg and the whole thing must have been agony for him. I got into the driver's seat beside him.

"The rope," I said. "We left it behind."

"Forget it," he said. "It doesn't matter."

I started the motor and switched on the headlights. I backed the car and turned it around and soon we were heading downhill on the bumpy track.

"Go slowly, Danny," my father said. "It hurts like crazy over the bumps." He had one hand on the wheel, helping to guide the car.

We reached the bottom of the track and turned onto the road.

"You're doing fine," he said. "Keep going."

Now that we were on the main road, I changed into second gear.

"Rev her up and go into third," he said. "Do you want me to help you?"

"I think I can do it," I said.

I changed into third gear.

With my father's hand on the wheel I had no fear of hitting the hedge or anything else, so I pressed down hard on the accelerator. The speedometer needle crept up to forty.

Something big with headlights blazing came rushing toward us. "I'll take the wheel," my father said. "Let go of it completely." He kept the little car close in to the side of the road as a huge milk truck rushed past us. That was the only thing we met on the way home.

As we approached the filling station my father said, "I'll have to go to the hospital for this. It must be set properly and then put into plaster."

"How long will you be in the hospital?"

"Don't worry, I'll be home before evening."

"Will you be able to walk?"

"Yes. They fix a metal thing into the plaster. It sticks out underneath the foot. I'll be able to walk on that."

"Should we go to the hospital now?"

"No," he said. "I'll just lie down on the floor of the workshop and wait till it's time to call Doc Spencer. He'll arrange everything."

"Call him now," I said.

"No. I don't like waking doctors up at four thirty in the morning. We'll call him at seven."

"What will you tell him, dad? I mean about how it happened?"

"I'll tell him the truth," my father said. "Doc Spencer is my friend."

We pulled into the filling station, and I parked the car right up against the workshop doors. I helped my father to get out. Then I held him around the waist as he hop-hopped the short distance into the workshop.

Inside the workshop, he leaned against the tool bench for support and told me what to do next.

First, I spread some sheets of newspaper out over the oily floor. Then I ran to the caravan and fetched two blankets and a pillow. I laid one blanket on the floor over the newspaper. I helped my father to lie down on the blanket. Then I put the pillow under his head and covered him up with the second blanket.

"Put the phone down here so I can reach it," he said.

I did as he asked.

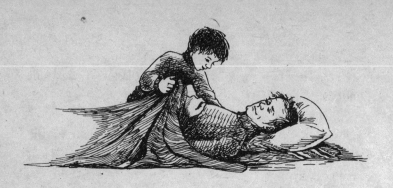

"Can I get you anything, dad? What about a hot drink?"

"No, thank you," he said. "I mustn't have a thing. I'm going to have an anesthetic soon, and you mustn't eat or drink anything at all before that. But *you* have something. Go and make yourself some breakfast. Then go to bed."

"I'd like to wait here till the doctor comes," I said.

"You must be dead tired, Danny."

"I'm all right," I said.

I found an old wooden chair and pulled it up near him and sat down.

He closed his eyes and seemed to be dozing off.

My own eyes kept closing, too. I couldn't keep them open.

"I'm sorry about the mess I made of it all," I heard him saying.

I must have gone to sleep after that because the next thing I heard was Doc Spencer's voice saying to my father, "Well, my goodness me, William, what on earth have you been up to?"

I opened my eyes and saw the doctor bending down over my father, who was still lying on the floor of the workshop.

9

Doc Spencer

MY FATHER ONCE TOLD ME that Doc Spencer had been look-ing after the people of our district for nearly forty-five years. He was over seventy now and could have retired long ago, but he didn't want to retire, and his patients didn't want him to either. He was a tiny man with tiny hands and feet and a tiny round face. The face was as brown and wrinkled as a shriveled apple. He was some sort of an elf, I used to think to myself each time I saw him, a very ancient sort of an elf with wispy white hair and steel-rimmed spectacles; a quick, clever little elf with a swift eye and a flashing smile and a fast way of talking. Nobody feared him. Many people loved him, and he was especially gentle with children.

"Which ankle?" he asked.

"The left one," my father said.

Doc Spencer knelt on the floor and took from his bag a pair of large scissors. Then to my astonishment he proceeded to slit the cloth of my father's left trouser-leg right up to the knee. He parted the cloth and looked at the ankle but he didn't touch it. I looked at it, too. The foot seemed to be

bent around sideways, and there was a huge swelling below the ankle bone.

"That's a nasty one," Doc Spencer said. "We'd better get you into the hospital right away. May I use your phone?"

He called the hospital and asked for an ambulance. Then he spoke to someone else about taking X-rays and doing an operation.

"How's the pain?" Doc Spencer asked. "Would you like me to give you something?"

"No," my father said. "I'll wait till I get there."

"As you wish, William. But how on earth did you do it? Did you fall down the steps of that crazy caravan?"

"Not exactly," my father said. "No."

The doctor waited for him to go on. So did I.

"As a matter of fact," he said slowly, "I was mooching around up in Hazell's Wood . . ." He paused again and looked at the doctor who was still kneeling beside him.

"Ah," the doctor said. "Yes, I see. And what's it like up there these days? Plenty of pheasants?"

"Stacks of them," my father said.

"It's a great game," Doc Spencer said, sighing a little. "I only wish I was young enough to have another go at it." He looked up and saw me staring at him. "You didn't know I used to do a bit of poaching myself, did you, Danny?"

"No," I said, absolutely flabbergasted.

"Many a night," Doc Spencer went on, "after evening surgery was over, I used to slip out the back door and go striding over the fields to one of my secret places. Sometimes it was pheasants and other times it was trout. Plenty of big brown trout in the stream in those days."

He was still kneeling on the floor beside my father. "Try not to move," he said to him. "Lie quite still."

My father closed his tired eyes, then opened them again. "Which method did you use for pheasants?" he asked.

"Gin and raisins," Doc Spencer said. "I used to soak the raisins in gin for a week, then scatter them in the woods."

"It doesn't work," my father said.

"I know it doesn't," the doctor said. "But it was enormous fun."

"One single pheasant," my father said, "has got to eat at least sixteen gin-soaked raisins before he gets tiddly enough for you to catch him. My own dad proved that with roosters."

"I believe you," the doctor said. "That's why I never caught any. But I was hot stuff with trout. Do you know how to catch a trout, Danny, without using a rod and line?"

"No," I said. "How?"

"You tickle him."

"*Tickle* him?"

"Yes," the doctor said. "Trout, you see, like to lie close in to the river bank. So you go creeping along the bank until you see a big one—and you come up behind him—and you lie down on your tummy—and then slowly, very slowly, you lower your hand into the water behind him—and you slide it underneath him—and you begin to stroke his belly up and down with the tip of one finger—"

"Will he really let you do that?" I asked.

"He loves it," the doctor said. "He loves it so much he sort of dozes off. And as soon as he dozes off, you quickly grab hold of him and flip him out of the water onto the bank."

"That works," my father said. "But only a great artist can do it. I take my hat off to you, sir."

"Thank you, William," Doc Spencer said gravely. He got up off his knees and crossed over to the door of the workshop and looked out to see if the ambulance was coming. "By the way," he said over his shoulder, "what happened up there in the woods? Did you step in a rabbit hole?"

"It was a slightly bigger hole than that," my father said.

"What do you mean?"

My father began to describe how he had fallen into the enormous pit.

Doc Spencer spun around and stared down at my father.

"I don't believe it!" he cried.

"It's perfectly true. Ask Danny."

"It was deep," I said. "Horribly deep."

"But great heavens alive!" the little doctor shouted, jumping up and down with fury. "He can't do that! Victor Hazell can't go digging tiger traps in his woods for human beings! I've never heard such a disgusting, monstrous thing in all my life!"

"It's rotten," my father said.

"It's worse than that, William! It's diabolical! Do you know what this means? It means that decent folk like you and me can't even go out and have a little fun at night without risking a broken leg or arm. We might even break our necks!"

My father nodded.

"I never did like that Victor Hazell," Doc Spencer said. "I saw him do a filthy thing once."

"What?" my father asked.

"He had an appointment with me at my surgery. He needed an injection of some sort, I've forgotten what. Anyway, just by chance I was looking out the window as he drove up to my door in his whacking great Rolls-Royce. I saw him get out, and I also saw my old dog Bertie dozing on the doorstep. And do you know what this loathsome Victor Hazell did? Instead of stepping over old Bertie, he actually kicked him out of the way with his riding boot."

"He didn't!" my father said.

"Oh, yes he did."

"What did you do?"

"I left him sitting in the waiting room while I picked out the oldest, bluntest needle I could find. Then I rubbed the point of it on a nail file to make it blunter still. By the time I'd got through with it, it was blunter than a ballpoint pen. Then I called him in and told him to lower his pants and bend over, and when I rammed that needle into his fleshy backside, he screamed like a stuck pig."

"Hooray," my father said.

"He's never been back since," Doc Spencer said. "For which I am truly thankful. Ah, here's the ambulance."

The ambulance drew up near the workshop door, and two men in uniform got out. "Bring me a leg splint," the doctor said. One of the men fetched a sort of thin wooden plank from the ambulance. Doc Spencer knelt down once more beside my father and eased the plank very gently underneath my father's left leg. Then he strapped the leg firmly to the plank. The ambulance men brought in a stretcher and placed it on the ground. My father got onto it by himself.

I was still sitting on my chair. Doc Spencer came over to me and put a hand on my shoulder. "I think you had better come on home with me, young man," he said. "You can stay with us until your father's back from the hospital."

"Won't he be home today?" I asked.

"Yes," my father said. "I'll be back this evening."

"I'd rather you stayed in for the night," Doc Spencer said.

"I shall come home this evening," my father said. "Thank you for offering to take Danny, but it won't be necessary.

He'll be all right here until I get back. I reckon he'll sleep most of the day anyway, won't you, my love?"

"I think so," I said.

"Just close up the filling station and go to bed, right?"

"Yes, but come back soon, won't you, dad?"

They carried him into the ambulance on the stretcher and closed the doors. I stood outside the workshop with Doc Spencer and watched the big white thing drive out of the filling station.

"Do you need any help?" Doc Spencer said.

"I'm fine, thank you."

"Go to bed, then, and get a good sleep."

"Yes, I will."

"Call me if you need anything."

"Yes."

The marvelous little doctor got into his car and drove away down the road in the same direction as the ambulance.

10

The Great Shooting Party

AS SOON AS THE doctor had driven away from the filling station, I went into the office and got out the sign that said SORRY CLOSED. I hung it on one of the pumps. Then I headed straight for the caravan. I was too tired to undress. I didn't even take off my dirty old sneakers. I just flopped down on the bunk and went to sleep. The time was five minutes past eight in the morning.

More than ten hours later, at six thirty in the evening, I was woken up by the ambulance men bringing my father back from the hospital. They carried him into the caravan and laid him on the lower bunk.

"Hello, dad," I said.

"Hello, Danny."

"How are you feeling?"

"A bit whoozy," he said, and he dozed off almost immediately.

As the ambulance men drove away, Doc Spencer arrived and went into the caravan to take a look at the patient. "He'll sleep until tomorrow morning," he said. "Then he'll wake up feeling fine."

I followed the doctor out to his car. "I'm awfully glad he's home," I said.

The doctor opened the car door but he didn't get in. He looked at me very sternly and said, "When did you last have something to eat, Danny?"

"Something to eat?" I said. "Oh—well—I had—er—" Suddenly I realized how long it had been. I hadn't eaten anything since I had had supper with my father the night before. That was nearly twenty-four hours ago.

Doc Spencer reached into the car and came out with something huge and round wrapped up in waxed paper. "My wife asked me to give you this," he said. "I think you'll like it. She's a fine cook."

He pushed the package toward me, then he jumped into the car and drove quickly away.

I stood there clasping the big round thing tightly in my hands. I watched the doctor's car as it went down the road and disappeared around the curve, and after it had gone I still stood there watching the empty road.

After a while I turned and walked back up the steps into the caravan with my precious parcel. I placed it in the center of the table but I didn't unwrap it.

My father lay on the bunk in a deep sleep. He was wearing hospital pajamas. They had brown and blue stripes. I went over and gently pulled back the blanket to see what they had done to him. Hard white plaster covered the lower part of his leg and the whole of his foot, except for the toes. There was a funny little iron thing sticking out below his foot, pre-

sumably for him to walk on. I covered
him up again and returned to the table.

Very carefully, I now began to unwrap
the waxed paper from around the doctor's
present, and when I had finished, I saw
before me the most enormous and beautiful pie in the world. It was covered all
over, top, sides, and bottom, with rich
golden pastry. I took a knife from
beside the sink and cut out a wedge.
I started to eat it in my fingers, standing up. It was a cold meat pie. The
meat was pink and tender with no
fat or gristle in it, and there were
hard-boiled eggs buried like treasures
in several different places. The taste
was absolutely fabulous. When I had
finished the first slice, I cut another
and ate that, too. God bless Doctor

Spencer, I thought. And God bless Mrs. Spencer as well.

The next morning, a Monday, my father
was up at six o'clock. "I feel great," he said. He
started hobbling around the caravan to test his
leg. "It hardly hurts at all!" he cried. "I can
walk you to school!"

"No," I said. "No."

"I've never missed one yet, Danny."

"It's two miles each way," I said. "Don't do it, dad, please."

So that day I went to school alone. But he insisted on coming with me the next day. I couldn't stop him. He had put a woolen sock over his plaster foot to keep his toes warm, and there was a hole in the underneath of the sock so that the metal thing could poke through. He walked a bit stiff-legged, but he moved as fast as ever, and the metal thing went *clink* on the road each time he put it down.

And so life at the filling station returned to normal, or anyway *nearly* to normal. I say "nearly" because things were definitely not quite the same as they had been before. The difference lay in my father. A change had come over him. It wasn't a big change, but it was enough to make me certain that something was worrying him quite a lot. He would brood a good deal, and there would be silences between us, especially at suppertime. Now and again I would see him standing alone and very still out in front of the filling station, gazing up the road in the direction of Hazell's Wood.

Many times I wanted to ask him what the trouble was and had I done so, I'm sure he would have told me at once. In any event, I knew that sooner or later I would hear all about it.

I hadn't long to wait.

About ten days after his return from the hospital, the two of us were sitting out on the platform of the caravan watching the sun go down behind the big trees on the top of the hill across the valley. We had had our supper, but it wasn't my bedtime yet. The September evening was warm and beautiful and very still.

"You know what makes me so hopping mad," he said to me all of a sudden. "I get up in the mornings feeling pretty good. Then around nine o'clock every single day of the week, that huge silver Rolls-Royce comes swishing past the filling station and I see the great big bloated face of Mr. Victor Hazell behind the wheel. I always see it. I can't help it. And as he passes by, he always turns his head in my direction and looks

at me. But it's the *way* he looks at me that is so infuriating. There is a sneer under his nose and a smug little smirk around his mouth, and although I only see him for three seconds, it makes me madder than mackerel. What's more, I stay mad for the rest of the day."

"I don't blame you," I said.

A silence fell between us. I waited to see what was coming next.

"I'll tell you something interesting," he said at last. "The shooting season for pheasants starts on Saturday. Did you know that?"

"No, dad, I didn't."

"It always starts on the first of October," he said. "And every year Mr. Hazell celebrates the occasion by giving a grand opening-day shooting party."

I wondered what this had to do with my father being madder than a mackerel, but I knew for certain there would be a connection somewhere.

"It is a very famous event, Danny, that shooting party of Mr. Hazell's."

"Do lots of people come?" I asked.

"Hundreds," he said. "They come from miles around. Dukes and lords, barons and baronets, wealthy businessmen, and all the fancy folk in the county. They come with their guns and their dogs and their wives, and all day long the noise of shooting rolls across the valley. But they don't come because they like Mr. Hazell. Secretly they all despise him. They think he's a nasty piece of work."

"Then why do they come, dad?"

"Because it's the best pheasant shoot in the South of England, that's why they come. But to Mr. Hazell it's the greatest day in the year, and he is willing to pay almost anything to make it a success. He spends a fortune on those pheasants. Each summer he buys hundreds of young birds from the pheasant farm and puts them in the wood where the keepers feed them and guard them and fatten them up ready for the great day to arrive. Do you know, Danny, that

the cost of rearing and keeping one single pheasant up to the time when it's ready to be shot is equal to the price of one hundred loaves of bread!"

"It's not true."

"I swear it," my father said. "But to Mr. Hazell it's worth every penny of it. And you know why? It makes him feel important. For one day in the year he becomes a big cheese in a little world and even the Duke of so-and-so slaps him on the back and tries to remember his first name when he says good-bye."

My father reached out a hand and scratched the hard plaster just below his left knee. "It itches," he said. "The skin itches underneath the plaster. So I scratch the plaster and pretend I'm scratching the skin."

"Does that help?"

"No," he said, "it doesn't help. But listen, Danny . . ."

"Yes, dad?"

"I want to tell you something."

He started scratching away again at the plaster on his leg. I waited for him to go on.

"I want to tell you what I would dearly love to do right now."

Here it comes, I thought. Here comes something big and crazy. I could tell something big and crazy was coming simply from watching his face.

"It's a deadly secret, Danny." He paused and looked carefully all around him. And although there was probably not a living person within two miles of us at that moment, he now leaned close to me and lowered his voice to a soft whisper. "I would like," he whispered, "to find a way of poaching so many pheasants from Hazell's Wood that there wouldn't be any left for the big opening-day shoot on October the first."

"Dad!" I cried. "No!"

"Ssshh," he said. "Listen. If only I could find a way of knocking off a couple of hundred birds all in one go, then Mr. Hazell's party would be the biggest washout in history!"

"Two hundred!" I said. *"That's impossible!"*

"Just imagine, Danny," he went on, "what a triumph, what a glorious victory that would be! All the dukes and lords and famous men would arrive in their big cars—and Mr. Hazell would strut about like a peacock welcoming them and saying things like, 'Plenty of birds out there for you this year, Lord Thistlethwaite,' and, 'Ah, my dear Sir Godfrey, this is a great season for pheasants, a very great season indeed'—and then out they would all go with their guns under their arms—and they would take up their positions surrounding the famous wood—and inside the wood a whole army of hired beaters would start shouting and yelling and bashing away at the undergrowth to drive the pheasants out of the wood toward the waiting guns—and lo and behold—there wouldn't be a single pheasant to be found anywhere! And Mr. Victor Hazell's face would be redder than a boiled beetroot! Now wouldn't that be the most amazing and beautiful thing if we could pull it off, Danny?"

My father had gotten himself so worked up that he rose

to his feet and hobbled down the caravan steps and started pacing back and forth in front of me. "Wouldn't it, though?" he shouted. "Wouldn't it be beautiful?"

"Yes," I said.

"But how?" he cried. "How could it be done?"

"There's no way, dad. It's hard enough getting just *two* birds up in those woods, let alone *two hundred*."

"I know that," my father said. "It's the keepers that make it so difficult."

"How many are there?" I asked.

"Keepers? Three, and they're always around."

"Do they stay right through the night?"

"No, not through the night," my father said. "They go off home as soon as all the pheasants are safely up in the trees, roosting. But nobody's ever discovered a way of poaching a roosting pheasant, not even my own dad who was the greatest expert in the world. It's about your bedtime," he added. "Off you go, and I'll come in and tell you a story."

11

~

The Sleeping Beauty

FIVE MINUTES LATER, I was lying on my bunk in my pajamas. My father came in and lit the oil lamp hanging from the ceiling. It was getting dark earlier now.

"All right," he said. "What sort of story shall we have tonight?"

"Dad," I said. "Wait a minute."

"What is it?"

"Can I ask you something? I've just had a bit of an idea."

"Go on," he said.

"You know that bottle of sleeping pills Doc Spencer gave you when you came back from the hospital?"

"I never used them. Don't like the things."

"Yes, but is there any reason why those wouldn't work on a pheasant?"

My father shook his head sadly from side to side.

"Wait," I said.

"It's no use, Danny. No pheasant in the world is going to swallow those lousy red capsules. Surely you know that."

"You're forgetting the raisins, dad."

"The raisins? What's that got to do with it?"

"Now listen," I said. "Please listen. We take a raisin. We soak it till it swells. Then we make a tiny slit in one side of it with a razor blade. Then we hollow it out a little. Then we open up one of your red capsules and pour all the powder into the raisin. Then we get a needle and thread and very carefully we sew up the slit . . ."

Out of the corner of my eye, I saw my father's mouth slowly beginning to open.

"Now," I said. "We have a nice clean-looking raisin chock full of sleeping-pill powder and that ought to be enough to put any pheasant to sleep. Don't you think so?"

My father was staring at me with a look of such wonder in his eyes he might have been seeing a vision.

"Oh, my darling boy," he said softly. "Oh, my sainted aunt! I do believe you've got it. Yes, I do—I do—I do."

He was suddenly so choked up with excitement that for a few seconds he couldn't say any more. He came and sat on the edge of my bunk and there he stayed, nodding his head very slowly up and down.

"You really think it would work?" I asked him.

"Yes," he said quietly. "It'll work all right. With this method we could prepare *two hundred* raisins, and all we'd have to do is scatter them around the feeding grounds at sunset, and then walk away. Half an hour later, after it was dark and the keepers had all gone home, we would go back into the wood—and the pheasants would be up in the trees by then, roosting—and the pills would be beginning to work—and the pheasants would be starting to feel groggy—

they'd be wobbling and trying to keep their balance—and soon every pheasant that had eaten one *single raisin* would topple over unconscious and fall to the ground. Why, they'd be dropping out of the trees like apples! And all we'd have to do is walk around picking them up!"

"Can I do it with you, dad?"

"And they'd never catch us, either," my father said, not hearing me. "We'd simply stroll through the woods dropping a few raisins here and there as we went, and even if they were *watching* us, they wouldn't notice anything."

"Dad," I said, raising my voice, "you *will* let me come with you?"

"Danny, my love," he said, laying a hand on my knee and gazing at me with eyes large and bright as two stars, "if this thing works, it will *revolutionize* poaching."

"Yes, dad, but can I come with you?"

"Come with me?" he said, floating out of his dream at last. "But, my dear boy, of course you can come with me! It's your idea! You must be there to see it happening! Now then," he cried, bouncing up off the bed, "where are those pills?"

The small bottle of red capsules was standing beside the sink. It had been there ever since my father returned from the hospital. He fetched it and unscrewed the cap and poured the capsules onto my blanket. "Let's count them," he said.

We counted them together. There were exactly fifty.

"That's not enough," he said. "We need two hundred at

least." Then he cried out, "Wait! Hold it! There's no problem!" He began carefully putting the capsules back into the bottle and as he did so, he said, "All we've got to do, Danny, is divide the powder from one capsule among four raisins. In other words, quarter the dose. That way we would have enough to fill two hundred raisins."

"But would a quarter of one of those pills be strong enough to put a pheasant to sleep?" I asked.

"Of course it would, my dear boy. Work it out for yourself. How much smaller is a pheasant than a man?"

"Many, many times smaller."

"There you are, then. If one pill is enough to put a fully grown man to sleep, you'll only need a tiny bit of that for a pheasant. What we're giving him will knock the old pheasant for a loop! He won't know what's hit him!"

"But dad, two hundred raisins aren't going to get you two hundred pheasants."

"Why not?"

"Because the greediest birds are surely going to gobble up about ten raisins each."

"You've got a point there," my father said. "You certainly have. But somehow I don't think it will happen that way. Not if I'm very careful and spread them out over a wide area. Don't worry about it, Danny. I'm sure I can work it."

"And you promised I can come with you?"

"Absolutely," he said. "And we shall call this method *The Sleeping Beauty*. It will be a landmark in the history of poaching!"

I sat very still in my bunk, watching my father as he put each capsule back into the bottle. I could hardly believe what was happening, that we were really going to do it, that he and I alone were going to try to swipe practically the entire flock of Mr. Victor Hazell's prize pheasants. Just thinking about it sent little shivers of electricity running all over my skin.

"Exciting, isn't it?" my father said.

"I don't dare think about it, dad. It makes me shiver all over."

"Me too," he said. "But we must keep very calm from now on. We must make our plans very very carefully. Today is Wednesday. The shooting party is next Saturday."

"Cripes!" I said. "That's in three days' time! When do you and I go up to the wood and do the job?"

"The night before," my father said. "On the Friday. In that way they won't discover that all the pheasants have disappeared until it's too late and the party has begun."

"Friday's the day after tomorrow! My goodness, dad, we'll have to hurry if we're going to get two hundred raisins ready before then!"

My father stood up and began pacing the floor of the caravan. "Here's the plan of action," he said. "Listen carefully. . . .

"Tomorrow is Thursday. When I walk you to school, I shall go into Stevens Stores in the village and buy two packets of seedless raisins. And in the evening we will put the raisins in to soak for the night."

"But that only gives us Friday to get ready two hundred raisins," I said. "Each one will have to be cut open and filled with powder and sewed up again. And I'll be at school all day. . . ."

"No, you won't," my father said. "You will be suffering from a very nasty cold on Friday and I shall be forced to keep you home from school."

"Hooray!" I said.

"We will not open the filling station at all on Friday," he went on. "Instead we will shut ourselves in here and prepare the raisins. We'll easily get them done between us in one day. And that evening, off we shall go up the road toward the wood to do the job. Is that all clear?"

He was like a general announcing the plan of battle to his staff.

"All clear," I said.

"And, Danny, not a whisper of this to any of your friends at school."

"Dad, you know I wouldn't!"

He kissed me good night and turned the oil lamp down low, but it was a long time before I went to sleep.

12

∾

Thursday and School

THE NEXT DAY WAS Thursday, and before we set out for the walk to my school that morning, I went around behind the caravan and picked two apples from our tree, one for my father and one for me.

It is a most marvelous thing to be able to go out and help yourself to your own apples whenever you feel like it. You can do this only in the autumn, of course, when the fruit is ripe, but all the same, how many families are so lucky? Not one in a thousand, I would guess. Our apples were called Cox's Orange Pippins, and I liked the sound of the name almost as much as I liked the apples.

At eight o'clock we started walking down the road toward my school in the pale autumn sunshine, munching our apples as we strode along.

Clink went my father's iron foot each time he put it down on the hard road. *Clink . . . clink . . . clink*.

"Have you brought money to buy the raisins?" I asked.

He put a hand in his trouser pocket and made the coins jingle.

"Will Stevens be open so early?"

"Yes," he said. "They open at eight thirty."

I really loved those morning walks to school with my father. We talked practically the whole time. Mostly it was he who talked and I who listened, and just about everything he said was fascinating. He was a true countryman. The fields, the streams, the woods, and all the creatures who lived in these places were a part of his life. Although he was a mechanic by trade, and a very fine one, I believe he could have become a great naturalist if only he had had a good schooling.

Long ago he had taught me the names of all the trees and the wildflowers and the different grasses that grow in the fields. All the birds, too, I could name, not only by sighting them but by listening to their calls and their songs.

In springtime we would hunt for birds' nests along the way, and when we found one he would lift me up onto his shoulders so I could peer into it and see the eggs. But I was never allowed to touch them.

My father told me a nest with eggs in it was one of the most beautiful things in the world. I thought so too. The nest of a song thrush, for instance, lined inside with dry mud as smooth as polished wood and with five eggs of the purest blue, speckled with black dots. And the skylark, whose nest we once found right in the middle of a meadow, in a grassy clump on the ground. It was hardly a nest at all, just a little hollow place in the grass, and in it were six small eggs, deep brown and white.

"Why does the skylark make its nest on the ground where the cows can trample it?" I asked.

"Nobody knows why," my father said. "But they always do it. Nightingales nest on the ground, too. So do pheasants and partridges and grouse."

On one of our walks a weasel flashed out of the hedge in front of us, and in the next few minutes I learned a lot of things about that marvelous little creature. The bit I liked best was when he said, "The weasel is the bravest of all the animals. The mother will fight to the death to defend her own children. She will never run away, not even from a fox which is one hundred times bigger than her. She will stay beside her nest and fight the fox until she is killed."

Another time, when I said, "Just listen to that grasshopper, dad," he said, "No, that's not a grasshopper, my love. It's a cricket. And did you know that crickets have their ears in their legs?"

"It's not true."

"It's absolutely true. And grasshoppers have theirs in the sides of their tummies. They are lucky to be able to hear at all because nearly all the vast hordes of insects on this earth are deaf as well as dumb and live in a silent world."

On this Thursday, on this particular walk to school, there was an old frog croaking in the stream behind the hedge as we went by.

"Can you hear him, Danny?"

"Yes," I said.

"That is a bullfrog calling to his wife. He does it by

blowing out his dewlap and letting it go with a burp."

"What is a dewlap?" I asked.

"It's the loose skin on his throat. He can blow it up just like a little balloon."

"What happens when his wife hears him?"

"She goes hopping over to him. She is very happy to have been invited. But I'll tell you something very funny about the old bullfrog. He often becomes so pleased with the sound of his own voice that his wife has to nudge him several times before he'll stop his burping and turn around to hug her."

That made me laugh.

"Don't laugh too loud," he said, twinkling at me with his eyes. "We men are not so very different from the bullfrog."

We parted at the school gates, and my father went off to buy the raisins. Other children were streaming in through the gates and heading up the path to the front door of the school. I joined them but kept silent. I was the keeper of a deep secret, and a careless word from me could blow the lid off the greatest poaching expedition the world would ever see.

Ours was just a small village school, a squat ugly red-brick building with no upstairs rooms at all. Above the front door was a big gray block of stone cemented into the brickwork, and on the stone it said: THIS SCHOOL WAS ERECTED IN 1901 TO COMMEMORATE THE CORONATION OF HIS ROYAL HIGHNESS KING EDWARD THE SEVENTH. I must have read that thing a thousand times. Every time I went in the door it hit me in the eye. I suppose that's what it was there for. But it's pretty boring to read the same old words over and over again, and I often thought how nice it would be if they put something different up there every day, something really interesting. My father would have done it for them beautifully. He could have written it with a bit of chalk on the smooth gray stone, and each morning it would have been something new. He would have said things like, *Did you know that the little yellow clover butterfly often carries his wife around on his back?* Another time he might have said, *The guppy has funny habits. When he falls in love with another guppy, he bites her on the bottom.* And another time, *Did you know that the death's head moth can squeak?* And then again, *Birds have almost no sense of smell. But they have good eyesight and they love red colors. The flowers they like are red and yellow, but never blue.* And perhaps another time he would get out his chalk and write, *Some bees have tongues which they can unroll until they are nearly twice as long as the bee itself. This is to allow them to gather nectar from flowers that have very long, narrow openings.* Or he might have written, *I'll bet you didn't know that in some big English country houses, the butler still has to iron the morning newspaper before putting it on his master's breakfast table.*

There were about sixty boys and girls in our school, and their ages went from five to eleven. We had four classrooms and four teachers.

Miss Birdseye taught the kindergarten, the five-year-olds and six-year-olds, and she was a really nice person. She used to keep a bag of aniseed balls in the drawer of her desk, and anyone who did good work would be given one aniseed ball to suck right there and then during the lesson. The trick with aniseed balls is never to bite them. If you keep rolling them around your mouth, they will dissolve slowly of their own accord, and then, right in the very center, you will find a tiny little brown seed. This is the aniseed itself, and when you crush it between your teeth, it has a fabulous taste. My father told me that dogs go crazy about it. When there aren't any foxes around, the huntsman will drag a bag of aniseed for miles and miles over the countryside, and the foxhounds will follow the scent because they love it so. This is known as a drag hunt.

The seven- and eight-year-olds were taught by Mr. Corrado, and he was also a decent person. He was a very old teacher, probably sixty or more, but that didn't seem to stop him being in love with Miss Birdseye. We knew he was in love

with her because he always gave her the best bits of meat at lunch when it was his turn to do the serving. And when she smiled at him he would smile back at her in the soppiest way you can imagine, showing all his front teeth, top and bottom, and most of the others as well.

A teacher called Captain Lancaster took the nine- and ten-year-olds, and this year that included me. Captain Lancaster, known sometimes as "Lankers," was a horrid man. He had fiery carrot-colored hair and a little clipped carrotty moustache and a fiery temper. Carrotty-colored hairs also sprouted out of his nostrils and his earholes. He had been a captain 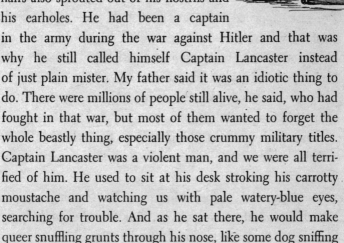 in the army during the war against Hitler and that was why he still called himself Captain Lancaster instead of just plain mister. My father said it was an idiotic thing to do. There were millions of people still alive, he said, who had fought in that war, but most of them wanted to forget the whole beastly thing, especially those crummy military titles. Captain Lancaster was a violent man, and we were all terrified of him. He used to sit at his desk stroking his carrotty moustache and watching us with pale watery-blue eyes, searching for trouble. And as he sat there, he would make queer snuffling grunts through his nose, like some dog sniffing around a rabbit hole.

Mr. Snoddy, our headmaster, took the top form, the eleven-year-olds, and everybody liked him. He was a small round man with a huge scarlet nose. I felt sorry for him having a nose like that. It was so big and inflamed it looked as though it might explode at any moment and blow him up.

A funny thing about Mr. Snoddy was that he always brought a glass of water with him into class, and this he kept sipping right through the lesson. At least everyone *thought* it was a glass of water. Everyone, that is, except me and my best friend, Sidney Morgan. We knew differently, and this is how we found out. My father looked after Mr. Snoddy's car, and I always took his repair bills with me to school to save postage. One day during intermission, I went to Mr. Snoddy's study to give him a bill and Sidney Morgan came along with me. He didn't come for any special reason. We just happened to be together at the time. And as we went in, we saw Mr. Snoddy standing by his desk refilling his famous glass of water from a bottle labeled GORDON'S GIN. He jumped a mile when he saw us.

"You should have knocked," he said, sliding the bottle behind a pile of books.

"I'm sorry, sir," I said. "I brought my father's bill."

"Ah," he said. "Yes. Very well. And what do *you* want, Sidney?"

"Nothing, sir," Sidney Morgan said. "Nothing at all."

"Off you go, then, both of you," Mr. Snoddy said, keeping his hand on the bottle behind the books. "Run along."

Outside in the corridor, we made a pact that we wouldn't tell any of the other children about what we had seen. Mr.

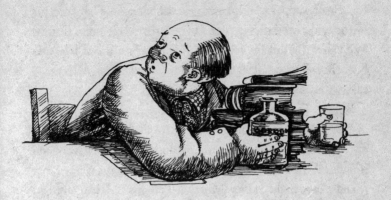

Snoddy had always been kind to us, and we wanted to repay him by keeping his deep dark secret to ourselves.

The only person I told was my father, and when he heard it, he said, "I don't blame him one bit. If I was unlucky enough to be married to Mrs. Snoddy, I would drink something a bit stronger than gin."

"What would you drink, dad?"

"Poison," he said. "She's a frightful woman."

"Why is she frightful?" I asked.

"She's a sort of witch," he said. "And to prove it, she has seven toes on each foot."

"How do you know that?" I asked.

"Doc Spencer told me," my father answered. And then to change the subject, he said, "Why don't you ever ask Sidney Morgan over here to play?"

Ever since I started going to school, my father had tried to encourage me to bring my friends back to the filling station for tea or supper. And every year, about a week before my birthday, he would say, "Let's have a party this time, Danny. We can write out invitations and I'll go into the village and buy chocolate éclairs and doughnuts and a huge birthday cake with candles on it."

But I always said no to these suggestions and I never invited any other children to come to my home after school or at weekends. That wasn't because I didn't have good friends. I had lots of them. Some of them were super friends, especially Sidney Morgan. Perhaps if I had lived in the same street as some of them, instead of way out in the country, things would have been different. But then again, perhaps they wouldn't. You see, the real reason I didn't want anyone else to come back and play with me was because I liked being alone with my father better.

By the way, something horrible happened on that Thursday morning after my father had left me at the school gate and gone off to buy the raisins. We were having our first lesson of the day with Captain Lancaster, and he had set us a whole bunch of multiplication problems to work out in our exercise books. I was sitting next to Sidney Morgan in the back row, and we were both slogging away. Captain Lancaster sat up front at his desk, gazing suspiciously around the class with his watery-blue eyes. And even from the back row I could hear him snorting and snuffling through his nose like a dog outside a rabbit hole.

Sidney Morgan covered his mouth with his hand and whispered very softly to me, "What are eight nines?"

"Seventy-two," I whispered back.

Captain Lancaster's finger shot out like a bullet and pointed straight at my face. "You!" he shouted. "Stand up!"

"Me, sir?" I said.

"Yes *you*, you blithering little idiot!"

I stood up.

"You were talking!" he barked. "What were you saying?" He was shouting at me as though I was a platoon of soldiers on the parade ground. "Come on, boy! Out with it!"

I stood still and said nothing.

"Are you refusing to answer me?" he shouted.

"Please, sir," Sidney said. "It was my fault. I asked him a question."

"Oh, you did, did you? Stand up!"

Sidney stood up beside me.

"And what exactly did you ask him?" Captain Lancaster said, speaking more quietly now and far more dangerously.

"I asked him what are eight nines," Sidney said.

"And I suppose *you* answered him?" Captain Lancaster said, pointing at me again. He never called any of us by our names. It was always "you" or "boy" or "girl" or something like that. "Did you answer him or didn't you? Speak up, boy!"

"Yes, sir," I said.

"So you were cheating!" he said. "Both of you were cheating!"

We kept silent.

"Cheating is a repulsive habit practiced by guttersnipes and dandyprats!" he said.

From where I was standing I could see the whole class sitting absolutely rigid, watching Captain Lancaster. Nobody dared move.

"You may be permitted to cheat and lie and swindle in your own homes," he went on, "but I will not put up with it here!"

At this point, a sort of blind fury took hold of me and I shouted back at him, "I am not a cheat!"

There was a fearful silence in the room. Captain Lancaster raised his chin and fixed me with his watery eyes. "You are not only a cheat but you are insolent," he said quietly. "You are a very insolent boy. Come up here. Both of you, come up here."

As I stepped out from my desk and began walking up toward the front of the class, I knew exactly what was going to happen. I had seen it happen to others many times, both to boys and girls. But up until now, it had never happened to me. Each time I had seen it, it had made me feel quite sick inside.

Captain Lancaster was standing up and crossing over to the tall bookcase that stood against the left-hand wall of the classroom. He reached up to the topmost shelf of the bookcase and brought down the dreaded cane. It was white, this cane, as white as bone, and very long and very thin, with one end bent over into a handle, like a walking stick.

"You first," he said, pointing at me with the cane. "Hold out your left hand."

It was almost impossible to believe that this man was about

to injure me physically and in cold blood. As I lifted my left palm upward and held it there, I looked at the palm itself and the pink skin and the fortune-teller's lines running over it, and I still could not bring myself to imagine that anything was going to happen to it.

The long white cane went up high in the air and came down on my hand with a crack like a rifle going off. I heard the crack first and about two seconds later I felt the pain. Never had I felt a pain such as that in my whole life. It was as though someone were pressing a red-hot poker against my palm and holding it there. I remember grabbing my injured left hand with my right hand and ramming it between my legs and squeezing my legs together against it. I squeezed

and squeezed as hard as I could, as if I were trying to stop the hand from falling to pieces. I managed not to cry out aloud but I couldn't keep the tears from pouring down my cheeks.

From somewhere nearby I heard another fearful *swish-crack* and I knew that poor Sidney had just gotten it as well.

But, oh, that fearful searing burning pain across my hand! Why didn't it go away? I glanced at Sidney. He was doing just the same as me, squeezing his hand between his legs and making the most awful face.

"Go and sit down, both of you!" Captain Lancaster ordered.

We stumbled back to our desks and sat down.

"Now get on with your work!" the dreaded voice said. "And let us have no more cheating! No more insolence, either!"

The class bent their heads over their books like people in church saying their prayers.

I looked at my hand. There was a long ugly mark about half an inch wide running right across the palm just where the fingers joined the hand. It was raised up in the middle and the raised part was pure white, with red on both sides. I moved the fingers. They moved all right, but it hurt to move them. I looked at Sidney. He gave me a quick apologetic glance under his eyelids, then went back to his work.

When I got home from school that afternoon, my father was in the workshop. "I've bought the raisins," he said. "We will now put them in to soak. Fetch me a bowl of water, Danny."

I went over to the caravan and got a bowl and half-filled it with water. I carried it to the workshop and put it on the bench.

"Open up the packets and tip them all in," my father said. This was one of the really nice things about my father. He didn't take over and want to do everything himself. Whether it was a difficult job like adjusting a carburetor in a big engine, or whether it was simply tipping some raisins into a basin, he always let me go ahead and do it myself while he watched and stood ready to help. He was watching me now as I opened the first packet of raisins.

"Hey!" he cried, grabbing my left wrist. "What's happened to your hand?"

"It's nothing," I said, clenching the fist.

He made me open it up. The long scarlet mark lay across my palm like a burn.

"Who did it?" he shouted. "Was it Captain Lancaster?"

"Yes, dad, but it's nothing."

"What happened?" He was gripping my wrist so hard it almost hurt. "Tell me exactly what happened!"

I told him everything. He stood there holding my wrist, his face going whiter and whiter, and I could see the fury beginning to boil up dangerously inside him.

"*I'll kill him!*" he whispered softly when I had finished. "*I swear I'll kill him!*" His eyes were blazing, and all the color had gone from his face. I had never seen him look like that before.

"Forget it, dad."

"I will not forget it!" he said. "You did nothing wrong, and he had absolutely no right to do this to you. So he called you a cheat, did he?"

I nodded.

He had taken his jacket from the peg on the wall and was putting it on.

"Where are you going?" I asked.

"I am going straight to Captain Lancaster's house and I'm going to beat the daylights out of him."

"No!" I cried, catching hold of his arm. "Don't do it, dad, please! It won't do any good! Please don't do it!"

"I've got to," he said.

"No!" I cried, tugging at his arm. "It'll ruin everything! It'll only make it worse! Please forget it!"

He hesitated. I held onto his arm. He was silent, and I could see the rush of anger slowly draining out of his face.

"It's revolting," he said.

"I'll bet they did it to you when you were at school," I said.

"Of course they did."

"And I'll bet your dad didn't go rushing off to beat the daylights out of the teacher who did it."

He looked at me but kept quiet.

"He didn't, did he, dad?"

"No, Danny, he didn't," he answered softly.

I let go of his arm and helped him off with his jacket and

hung it back on the peg.

"I'm going to put the raisins in now," I said. "And don't forget that tomorrow I have a nasty cold and I won't be going to school."

"Yes," he said. "That's right."

"We've got two hundred raisins to fill," I said.

"Ah," he said. "So we have."

"I hope we'll get them done in time," I said.

"Does it still hurt?" he asked. "That hand?"

"No," I said. "Not one bit."

I think that satisfied him. And although I saw him glancing occasionally at my palm during the rest of the afternoon and evening, he never mentioned the subject again.

That night he didn't tell me a story. He sat on the edge of my bunk, and we talked about what was going to happen the next day up in Hazell's Wood. He got me so steamed up and excited about it, I couldn't get to sleep. I think he must have gotten himself steamed up almost as much because after he had undressed and climbed into his own bunk, I heard him twisting and turning all over the place. He couldn't get to sleep either.

At about ten thirty, he climbed out of his bunk and put the kettle on.

"What's the matter, dad?"

"Nothing," he said. "Shall we have a midnight feast?"

"Yes, let's do that."

He lit the lamp in the ceiling and opened a can of salmon

and made a delicious sandwich for each of us. Also hot chocolate for me, and tea for him. Then we started talking about the pheasants and about Hazell's Wood all over again.

It was pretty late before we got to sleep.

13

Friday

WHEN MY FATHER woke me at six o'clock next morning, I knew at once that this was the day of days. It was the day I longed for and the day I dreaded. It was also the day of butterflies in the stomach, except that they were worse than butterflies. They were snakes. I had snakes in the stomach the moment I opened my eyes on that Friday morning.

The first thing I did after I had got dressed was to hang the SORRY CLOSED notice on one of the pumps. We had a quick breakfast, then the two of us sat down together at the table in the caravan to prepare the raisins. They were plump and soft and swollen from being soaked in water, and when you nicked them with a razor blade the skin sprang open and the jelly stuff inside squeezed out as easily as you could wish.

I slit the raisins while my father opened the capsules. He opened only one at a time and poured the white powder onto a piece of paper. Then he divided it into four tiny piles with the blade of a knife. Each pile was carefully scooped up and put into a single raisin. A needle and black cotton finished the job. The sewing up was the hardest part, and my father did most of that. It took about two minutes to do one raisin from start to finish. I enjoyed it. It was fun.

"Your mother was wonderful at sewing things," my father said. "She'd have had these raisins done in no time."

I didn't say anything. I never knew quite what to say when he talked about my mother.

"Did you know she used to make all my clothes herself, Danny? Everything I wore."

"Even socks and sweaters?" I asked.

"Yes," he said. "But those were knitted. And so quickly! When she was knitting, the needles flew so fast in her fingers you couldn't see them. They were just a blur. I would sit here in the evening watching her, and she used to talk about the children she was going to have. 'I shall have three children,' she used to say. 'A boy for you, a girl for me, and one for good measure.' "

There was a short silence after that. Then I said, "When mum was here, dad, did you go out very often at night or was it only now and then?"

"You mean poaching?"

"Yes."

"Often," he said. "At least twice a week."

"Didn't she mind?"

"Mind? Of course she didn't mind. She came with me."

"She didn't!"

"She certainly did. She came with me every single time until just before you were born. She had to stop then. She said she couldn't run fast enough."

I thought about this extraordinary piece of news for a little while. Then I said, "Was the only reason she went because she loved you, dad, and because she wanted to be with you? Or did she go because she loved poaching?"

"Both," my father said. "She did it for both the reasons you mentioned."

I was beginning to realize what an immense sorrow it must have been to him when she died.

"Weren't you afraid she might get shot up?" I asked.

"Yes, Danny, I was. But it was marvelous to have her along. She was a great sport, your mother."

By midday we had prepared one hundred and thirty-six raisins. "We're in good shape," my father said. "Let's break for lunch."

He opened a can of baked beans and heated them up in a saucepan over the kerosene burner. I cut two slices of brown bread and put them on plates. My father spooned the hot baked beans over the bread, and we carried our plates outside and sat down with our legs dangling over the platform of the caravan.

Usually I love baked beans on bread, but today I couldn't eat a thing. "What's the matter?" my father asked.

"I'm not hungry."

"Don't worry," he said. "The same thing happened to me the first time I went out. I was about your age then, maybe a little older, and in those days we always had a hot tea in the kitchen at five o'clock. I can remember exactly what was on the table that evening. It was my favorite thing of all, toad-in-the-hole, and my mum could make toad-in-the-hole like nobody else in the world. She did it in an enormous pan with the Yorkshire pudding very brown and crisp on top and raised up in huge bubbly mountains. In between the

mountains you could see the sausages half buried in the batter. Fantastic it was. But on that day my stomach was so jumpy I couldn't eat one mouthful. I expect yours feels like that now."

"Mine's full of snakes," I said. "They won't stop wiggling about."

"Mine doesn't feel exactly normal either," my father said. "But then, this isn't a normal operation, is it?"

"No, dad, it's not."

"Do you know what this is, Danny? This is the most colossal and extraordinary poaching job anyone has ever been on in the history of the world!"

"Don't go on about it, dad. It only makes me more jumpy. What time do we leave here?"

"I've worked that out," he said. "We must enter the wood about fifteen minutes before sunset. If we arrive after sunset, all the pheasants will have flown up to roost and it'll be too late."

"When is sunset?" I asked.

"Right now it's around seven thirty," he said. "So we must arrive at seven fifteen exactly. It's an hour and a half's walk to the wood so we must leave here at a quarter to six."

"Then we'd better finish those raisins," I said. "We've still got more than sixty to do."

We finished the raisins with about two hours to spare. They lay in a pile on a white plate in the middle of the table. "Don't they look marvelous?" my father said, rubbing his hands together hard. "Those pheasants are going to absolutely love them."

After that, we messed around in the workshop until half past five. Then my father said, "That's it! It's time to get ready! We leave in fifteen minutes!"

As we walked toward the caravan, a station wagon pulled up to the pumps with a woman at the wheel and about eight children in the back all eating ice cream.

"Oh, I know you're closed," the woman called out through her window. "But couldn't you please let me have a few gallons. I'm just about empty." She was a good-looking woman with dark hair.

"Give it to her," my father said. "But be quick."

I fetched the key from the office and unlocked one of the pumps. I filled up her tank and took the money and gave her the change. "You don't usually close as early as this," she said.

"We have to go out," I told her, hopping from one foot to the other. "I have to go somewhere with my father."

"You look jumpy as a jackrabbit," she said. "Is it the dentist?"

"No, ma'am," I said. "It's not the dentist. But please excuse me. I have to go now."

14

In the Wood

MY FATHER CAME OUT of the caravan wearing the old navy-blue sweater and the brown cloth cap with the peak pulled down low over his eyes.

"What's under there, dad?" I asked, seeing the bulge at his waistline.

He pulled up his sweater and showed me two thin but very large white cotton sacks. They were bound neat and tidy around his belly. "To carry the stuff," he said darkly.

"Ah-ha."

"Go and put on your sweater," he said. "It's brown, isn't it?"

"Yes," I said.

"That'll do. But take off those white sneakers and wear your black shoes instead."

I went into the caravan and changed my shoes and put on my sweater. When I came out again, my father was standing by the pumps squinting anxiously up at the sun which was now only the width of a man's hand above the line of trees along the crest of the ridge on the far side of the valley.

"I'm ready, dad."

"Good boy. Off we go!"

"Have you got the raisins?" I asked.

"In here," he said, tapping his trouser pocket where yet another bulge was showing. "I've put them all in one bag."

It was a calm sunny evening with little wisps of brilliant white cloud hanging motionless in the sky. The valley was cool and very quiet as the two of us began walking together along the road that ran between the hills toward Wendover. The iron thing underneath my father's foot made a noise like a hammer striking a nail each time it hit the road.

"This is it, Danny. We're on our way now," he said. "By golly, I wish my old dad were coming with us on this one. He'd have given his front teeth to be here at this moment."

"Mum, too," I said.

"Ah, yes," he said, giving a little sigh. "Your mother would have *loved* this one."

Then he said, "Your mother was a great one for walking, Danny. And she would always bring something home with her to brighten up the caravan. In summer it was wildflowers or grasses. When the grass was in seed she could make it look absolutely beautiful in a jug of water, especially with some stalks of wheat or barley in between. In the fall she would pick branches of leaves, and in the winter it was berries or old man's beard."

We kept going. Then he said, "How do you feel, Danny?"

"Terrific," I said. And I meant it. For although the snakes were still wiggling in my stomach, I wouldn't have swapped places with the King of Arabia at that moment.

"Do you think they might have dug any more of those pits for us to fall into?" I asked.

"Don't you go worrying about pits, Danny," my father said. "I'll be on the lookout for them this time. We shall go very carefully and very slowly once we're in the wood."

"How dark will it be in there when we arrive?"

"Not too dark," he said. "Quite light, in fact."

"Then how do we stop the keepers from seeing us?"

"Ah," he said. "That's the fun of the whole thing. That's what it's all about. It's hide and seek. It's the greatest game of hide and seek in the world."

"You mean because they've got guns?"

"Well," he said, "that does add a bit of a flavor to it, yes."

We didn't talk much after that. But as we got closer and closer to the wood, I could see my father becoming more and more twitchy as the excitement began to build up in him. He would get hold of some awful old tune and instead of using the words, he would go "Tum-tiddely-um-tum-tum-tum-tum" over and over again. Then he would get hold of another tune and go "Pom-piddely-om-pom-pom-pom-pom, pom-piddely-om, pom-piddely-om." As he sang, he tried to keep time with the tap-tap of his iron foot on the roadway.

When he got tired of that, he said to me, "I'll tell you something interesting about pheasants, Danny. The law says they're wild birds, so they only belong to you when they're on your own land. Did you know that?"

"I didn't know that, dad."

"So if one of Mr. Hazell's pheasants flew over and perched on our filling station," he said, "it would belong to us. No one else would be allowed to touch it."

"You mean even if Mr. Hazell had bought it himself as a chick?" I said. "Even if he had bought it and reared it in his own wood?"

"Absolutely," my father said. "Once it flies off his own land, he's lost it. Unless, of course, it flies back again. It's the same with fish. Once a trout or a salmon has swum out of your stretch of the river into somebody else's, you can't very well say, 'Hey, that's mine. I want it back,' can you?"

"Of course not," I said. "But I didn't know it was like that with pheasants."

"It's the same with all game," my father said. "Hare, deer, partridge, grouse. You name it."

We had been walking steadily for about an hour and a quarter and we were coming to the gap in the hedge where the cart track led up the hill to the big wood where the pheasants lived. We crossed over the road and went through the gap.

We walked on up the cart track and when we reached the crest of the hill we could see the wood ahead of us, huge and dark with the sun going down behind the trees and little sparks of gold shining through.

"No talking, Danny, once we're inside," my father said. "Keep very close to me and try not to go snapping any branches."

Five minutes later we were there. The wood skirted the edge of the track on the right-hand side with only the hedge between it and us. "Come on," my father said. "In we go." He slipped through the hedge on all fours and I followed.

It was cool and murky inside the wood. No sunlight came in at all. My father took me by the hand, and together we started walking forward between the trees. I was very grateful to him for holding my hand. I had wanted to take hold of his the moment we entered the wood, but I thought he might disapprove.

My father was very tense. He was picking his feet up high and putting them down gently on the brown leaves. He kept his head moving all the time, the eyes sweeping slowly from side to side, searching for danger. I tried doing the same, but soon I began to see a keeper behind every tree, so I gave it up.

We went on like this for maybe four or five minutes, going slowly deeper and deeper into the wood.

Then a large patch of sky appeared ahead of us in the roof of the forest, and I knew that this must be the clearing. My father had told me that the clearing was the place where the young birds were introduced into the wood in early July, where they were fed and watered and guarded by the keepers, and where many of them stayed from force of habit until the shooting began. "There's always plenty of pheasants in the clearing," my father had said.

"And keepers, dad?"

"Yes," he had said. "But there's thick bushes all around and that helps."

The clearing was about one hundred yards ahead of us. We stopped behind a big tree while my father let his eyes rove very slowly all around. He was checking each little shadow and every part of the wood within sight.

"We're going to have to crawl the next bit," he whispered,

letting go of my hand. "Keep close behind me all the time, Danny, and do exactly as I do. If you see me lie flat on my face, you do the same. Right?"

"Right," I whispered back.

"Off we go, then. This is it!"

My father got down on his hands and knees and started crawling. I followed. He moved surprisingly fast on all fours and I had quite a job to keep up with him. Every few seconds he would glance back at me to see if I was all right, and each time he did so, I gave him a nod and a smile.

We crawled on and on, and then at last we were kneeling safely behind a big clump of bushes right on the edge of the clearing. My father was nudging me with his elbow and pointing through the branches at the pheasants.

The place was absolutely alive with them. There must have been at least two hundred huge birds strutting around among the tree stumps.

"You see what I mean?" he whispered.

It was a fantastic sight, a sort of poacher's dream come true. And how close they were! Some of them were not ten paces from where we knelt. The hens were plump and creamy-brown. They were so fat their breast feathers almost brushed the ground as they walked. The cocks were slim and elegant, with long tails and brilliant red patches around the eyes, like scarlet spectacles. I glanced at my father. His face was transfixed in ecstasy. The mouth was slightly open and the eyes were sparkling bright as they stared at the pheasants.

"There's a keeper," he said softly.

I froze. At first I didn't even dare to look.

"Over there," my father whispered.

I mustn't move, I told myself. Not even my head.

"Look carefully," my father whispered. "Over the other side, by that big tree."

Slowly, I swiveled my eyeballs in the direction he indicated. Then I saw him.

"Dad!" I whispered.

"Don't move now, Danny. Stay well down."

"Yes but dad—"

"It's all right. He can't see *us*."

We crouched close to the ground, watching the keeper. He was a smallish man with a cap on his head and a big double-barreled shotgun under his arm. He never moved. He was like a little post standing there.

"Should we go?" I whispered.

The keeper's face was shadowed by the peak of his cap, but it seemed to me he was looking straight at us.

"Should we go, dad?"

"Hush," my father said.

Slowly, never taking his eyes from the keeper, he reached into his pocket and brought out a single raisin. He placed it in the palm of his right hand, and then, quickly, with a little flick of the wrist, he threw the raisin high into the air. I watched it as it went sailing over the bushes, and I saw it land within a yard of two hen birds standing beside an old tree stump. Both birds turned their heads sharply at the drop

of the raisin. Then one of them hopped over and made a
quick peck at the ground and that must have been it.

I looked at the keeper. He hadn't moved.

I could feel a trickle of cold sweat running down one side
of my forehead and across my cheek. I didn't dare lift a hand
to wipe it away.

My father threw a second raisin into the clearing . . . then
a third . . . and a fourth . . . and a fifth.

It takes guts to do that, I thought. Terrific guts. If I'd
been alone, I would never have stayed there for one second.
But my father was in a sort of poacher's trance. For him,
this was it. This was the moment of danger, the biggest
thrill of all.

He kept on throwing raisins into the clearing, swiftly,
silently, one at a time. Flick went his wrist, and up went the
raisin, high over the bushes, to land among the pheasants.

Then all at once, I saw the keeper turn away his head to
inspect the wood behind him.

My father saw it too. Quick as a flash, he pulled the bag
of raisins out of his pocket and tipped the whole lot into
the palm of his right hand.

"Dad!" I whispered. "Don't!"

But with a great sweep of the arm he flung the entire handful way over the bushes into the clearing.

They fell with a soft little patter, like raindrops on dry leaves, and every single pheasant in the place must have heard them fall. There was a flurry of wings and a rush to find the treasure.

The keeper's head flicked around as though there were a spring inside his neck. The birds were all pecking away madly at the raisins. The keeper took two quick paces forward, and for a moment I thought he was going in to investigate. But then he stopped, and his face came up and his eyes began traveling slowly around the edge of the clearing.

"Lie down flat!" my father whispered, "Stay there! Don't move an inch!"

I flattened my body against the ground and pressed one side of my face into the brown leaves. The soil below the leaves had a queer pungent smell, like beer. Out of one eye, I saw my father raise his head just a tiny bit to watch the keeper. He kept watching him.

"Don't you *love* this?" he whispered to me.

I didn't dare answer him.

We lay there for what seemed like a hundred years.

At last I heard my father whisper, "Panic's over. Follow me, Danny. But be extra careful, he's still there. *And keep down low all the time.*"

He started crawling away quickly on his hands and knees. I went after him. I kept thinking of the keeper who was somewhere behind us. I was very conscious of that keeper, and I was also very conscious of my own backside, and how it was sticking up in the air for all to see. I could understand now why "poacher's bottom" was a fairly common complaint in this business.

We went along on our hands and knees for about a hundred yards.

"Now run!" my father said.

We got to our feet and ran, and a few minutes later we came out through the hedge into the lovely open safety of the cart track.

"It went marvelously!" my father said, breathing heavily. "Didn't it go absolutely marvelously?" His face was scarlet and glowing with triumph.

"Did the keeper see us?" I asked.

"Not on your life!" he said. "And in a few minutes the sun will be going down and the birds will all be flying up to roost and that keeper will be sloping off home to his supper. Then all we've got to do is go back in again and help ourselves. We'll be picking them up off the ground like pebbles!"

He sat down on the grassy bank below the hedge. I sat down close to him. He put an arm around my shoulders and gave me a hug. "You did well, Danny," he said. "I'm proud of you."

15

The Keeper

WE SAT ON THE GRASSY bank below the hedge, waiting for darkness to fall. The sun had set now, and the sky was a pale smoke blue, faintly glazed with yellow. In the wood behind us the shadows and the spaces in between the trees were turning from gray to black.

"You could offer me anywhere in the world at this moment," my father said, "and I wouldn't go."

His whole face was glowing with happiness.

"We did it, Danny," he said, laying a hand gently on my knee. "We pulled it off. Doesn't that make you feel good?"

"Terrific," I said. "But it was a bit scary while it lasted."

"Ah, but that's what poaching's all about," he said. "It scares the pants off us. That's why we love it. Look, there's a hawk!"

I looked where he was pointed and saw a sparrow hawk hovering superbly in the darkening sky above the plowed field across the track.

"It's his last chance for supper tonight," my father said. "He'll be lucky if he sees anything now."

Except for the swift fluttering of its wings, the hawk remained absolutely motionless in the sky. It seemed to be suspended by some invisible thread, like a toy bird hanging from the ceiling. Then suddenly it folded its wings and plummeted toward the earth at an incredible speed. This was a sight that always thrillled me.

"What do you think he saw, dad?"

"A young rabbit perhaps," my father said. "Or a vole or a field mouse. None of them has a chance when there's a sparrow hawk overhead."

We waited to see if the hawk would fly up again. He didn't, which meant he had caught his prey and was eating it on the ground.

"How long does a sleeping pill take to work?" I asked.

"I don't know the answer to that one," my father said. "I imagine it's about half an hour."

"It might be different with pheasants though, dad."

"It might," he said. "We've got to wait a while anyway, to give the keepers time to go home. They'll be off as soon as it gets dark. I've brought an apple for each of us," he added, fishing into one of his pockets.

"A Cox's Orange Pippin," I said, smiling. "Thank you very much."

We sat there munching away.

"One of the nice things about a Cox's Orange Pippin," my father said, "is that the seeds rattle when it's ripe. Shake it and you can hear them rattling."

I shook my half-eaten apple. The seeds rattled.

"Look out!" he whispered sharply. "There's someone coming."

The man had appeared suddenly and silently out of the dusk and was quite close before my father saw him. "It's another keeper," he whispered. "Just sit tight and don't say a word."

We both watched the keeper as he came down the track toward us. He had a shotgun under his arm and there was a black Labrador walking at his heel. He stopped when he was a few paces away and the dog stopped with him and stayed behind him, watching us through the keeper's legs.

"Good evening," my father said, nice and friendly.

This one was a tall, bony man with a hard eye and a hard cheek and hard dangerous hands.

"I know you," he said, coming closer. "I know the both of you."

My father didn't answer this.

"You're from the filling station. Right?"

His lips were thin and dry with some sort of a brownish crust over them.

"You're from the filling station and that's your boy and you live in that filthy old caravan. Right?"

"What are we playing?" my father said. "Twenty questions?"

The keeper spat out a big gob of spit and I saw it go sailing through the air and land with a plop on a patch of dry dust six inches from my father's plaster foot. It looked like a little baby oyster lying there.

"Beat it," the man said. "Go on. Get out."

When he spoke, his upper lip lifted above the gum, and I could see a row of small discolored teeth. One of them was black. The others were brownish-yellow, like the seeds of a pomegranate.

"This happens to be a public footpath," my father said. "Kindly do not molest us."

The keeper shifted the gun from his left arm to his right.

"You're loiterin'," he said, "with intent to commit a nuisance. I could run you in for that."

"No you couldn't," my father said.

All this made me rather nervous.

"I see you broke your foot," the keeper said. "You didn't by any chance fall into a hole in the ground, did you?"

"It's been a nice walk, Danny," my father said, putting a hand on my knee, "but it's time we went home for our supper." He stood up and so did I. We wandered off down the track the way we had come, leaving the keeper standing there, and soon he was out of sight in the half darkness behind us.

"That's the head keeper," my father said. "His name is Rabbetts."

"Do we have to go home, dad?"

"Home!" my father cried. "My dear boy, we're just beginning! Come in here."

There was a gate on our right leading into a field and we climbed over it and sat down behind the hedge.

"Mr. Rabbetts is also due for his supper," my father said. "You mustn't worry about him."

We sat quietly behind the hedge waiting for the keeper to walk past us on his way home. A few stars were showing and a bright three-quarter moon was coming up over the hills behind us in the east.

"We have to be careful of that dog," my father said. "When they come by, hold your breath and don't move a muscle."

"Won't the dog smell us out anyway?" I asked.

"No," my father said. "There's no wind to carry the scent. Look out! Here they come! Don't move!"

The keeper came loping softly down the track with the dog padding quick and soft-footed at his heel. I took a deep breath and held it as they went by.

When they were some distance away, my father stood up and said, "It's all clear. He won't be coming back tonight."

"Are you sure?"

"I'm positive, Danny."

"What about the other one, the one in the clearing?"

"He'll be gone too."

"Mightn't one of them be waiting for us at the bottom of the track?" I asked. "By the gap in the hedge?"

"There wouldn't be any point in him doing that," my father said. "There's at least twenty different ways of reaching the road when you come out of Hazell's Wood. Mr. Rabbetts knows that."

We stayed behind the hedge for a few minutes more just to be on the safe side.

"Isn't it a marvelous thought, though, Danny," my father said, "that there's about two hundred pheasants at this very moment roosting up in those trees and already they're beginning to feel groggy. Soon they'll be falling out of the branches like raindrops!"

The three-quarter moon was well above the hills now and the sky was filled with stars as we climbed back over the gate and began walking up the track toward the wood.

16

≈

The Champion of the World

IT WAS NOT AS dark as I had expected it to be inside the wood this time. Little glints and glimmers from the brilliant moon outside shone through the leaves and gave the place a cold eerie look.

"I brought a light for each of us," my father said. "We're going to need it later on." He handed me one of those small pocket flashlights shaped like a fountain pen. I switched mine on. It threw a long narrow beam of surprising brightness, and when I moved it around it was like waving a very long white wand among the trees. I switched it off.

We started walking back toward the clearing where the pheasants had eaten the raisins.

"This," my father said, "will be the first time in the history of the world that anyone has even tried to poach roosting pheasants. Isn't it marvelous, though, to be able to walk around without worrying about keepers?"

"You don't think Mr. Rabbetts might have sneaked back again just to make sure?"

"Never," my father said. "He's gone home to his supper."

I couldn't help thinking that if *I* had been Mr. Rabbetts,

and if *I* had seen two suspicious-looking characters lurking just outside my precious pheasant wood, *I* certainly would not have gone home to *my* supper. My father must have sensed my fears because once again he reached out and took my hand in his, folding his long warm fingers around mine.

Hand in hand, we threaded our way through the trees toward the clearing. In a few minutes we were there. "Here's where we threw the raisins," my father said.

I peered through the bushes. The clearing lay pale and milky in the moonlight.

"What do we do next?" I asked.

"We stay here and wait," my father said. I could just make out his face under the peak of his cap, the lips pale, the cheeks flushed, the eyes shining bright.

"Are they all roosting, dad?"

"Yes. They're all around us. They don't go far."

"Could I see them if I shone my light up into the branches?"

"No," he said. "They go up pretty high and they hide in among the leaves."

We stood waiting for something to happen.

Nothing happened. It was very quiet there in the wood.

"Danny," my father said.

"Yes, dad?"

"I've been wondering how a bird manages to keep its balance sitting on a branch when it's asleep."

"I don't know," I said. "Why?"

"It's very peculiar," he said.

"What's peculiar?"

"It's peculiar that a bird doesn't topple off its perch as soon as it goes to sleep. After all, if *we* were sitting on a branch and we went to sleep, we would fall off at once, wouldn't we?"

"Birds have claws and long toes, dad. I expect they hold on with those."

"I know that, Danny. But I still don't understand why the toes keep gripping the perch once the bird is asleep. Surely everything goes limp when you fall asleep."

I waited for him to go on.

"I was just thinking," he said, "that if a bird can keep its balance when it's asleep, then surely there isn't any reason why the pills should make it fall down."

"It's doped," I said. "Surely it will fall down if it's doped."

"But isn't that simply a *deeper* sort of sleep?" he said. "Why should we expect it to fall down just because it's in a *deeper* sleep?"

There was a gloomy silence.

"I should have tested it with roosters," my father added. Suddenly the blood seemed to have drained right out of his cheeks. His face was so pale I thought he might be going to faint. "My dad would have tested it with roosters before he did anything else," he said.

At that moment there came a soft thump from the wood behind us.

"What was that?" I asked.

"Ssshh!"

We stood listening.

Thump!

"There's another!" I said.

It was a deep muffled sound as though a bag of sand had been dropped to the ground.

Thump!

"They're pheasants!" I cried.

"Wait!"

"They must be pheasants, dad!"

Thump! Thump!

"You may be right, Danny!"

We switched on our flashlights and ran toward the sounds.

"Where were they?" my father said.

"Over here, dad! Two of them were over here!"

"I thought they were this way. Keep looking! They can't be far!"

We searched for about a minute.

"Here's one!" my father called.

When I got to him he was holding a magnificent cock bird in both hands. We examined it closely with our flashlights.

"It's doped to high heaven," my father said. "It won't wake up for a week."

Thump!

"There's another!" I cried.

Thump! Thump!

"Two more!" my father yelled.

Thump!

Thump! Thump! Thump!

"Jeepers!" my father said.

Thump! Thump! Thump! Thump!

Thump! Thump!

All around us the pheasants were starting to rain down out of the trees. We began rushing around madly in the dark, sweeping the ground with our flashlights.

Thump! Thump! Thump! This lot fell almost on top of me. I was right under the tree as they came down and I found all three of them immediately—two cocks and a hen. They

were limp and warm, the feathers wonderfully soft in the hand.

"Where shall I put them, dad?" I called out.

"Lay them here, Danny! Just pile them up here where it's light."

My father was standing on the edge of the clearing with the moonlight streaming down all over him and a great bunch of pheasants in each hand. His face was bright, his

eyes big and bright and wonderful, and he was staring around him like a child who has just discovered that the whole world is made of chocolate.

Thump!
Thump! Thump!

"It's too many!" I said.

"It's beautiful!" he cried. He dumped the birds he was carrying and ran off to look for more.

Thump! Thump! Thump! Thump!
Thump!

It was easy to find them now. There were one or two

lying under every tree. I quickly collected six more, three in each hand, and ran back and dumped them with the others. Then six more. Then six more after that.

And still they kept falling.

My father was in a whirl of excitement now, dashing about like a mad ghost under the trees. I could see the beam of his flashlight waving around in the dark, and every time he found a bird he gave a little yelp of triumph.

Thump! Thump! Thump!

"Hey, Danny!" he shouted.

"Yes, I'm over here. What is it, dad?"

"What do you think the great Mr. Victor Hazell would say if he could see this?"

"Don't talk about it," I said.

For three or four minutes, the pheasants kept on falling. Then suddenly they stopped.

"Keep searching!" my father shouted. "There's plenty more on the ground!"

"Dad," I said, "don't you think we ought to get out while the going's good?"

"Never!" he shouted. "Not on your life!"

We went on searching. Between us we looked under every tree within a hundred yards of the clearing, north, south, east, and west, and I think we found most of them in the end. At the collecting point there was a pile of pheasants as big as a bonfire.

"It's a miracle," my father was saying. "It's an absolute miracle." He was staring at them in a kind of trance.

"Shouldn't we just take about six each and get out quick?" I said.

"I would like to count them, Danny."

"Dad! Not now!"

"I *must* count them."

"Can't we do that later?"

"One . . .

"Two . . .

"Three . . .

"Four . . ."

He began counting them very carefully, picking up each bird in turn and laying it carefully to one side. The moon was directly overhead now, and the whole clearing was brilliantly lit up. I felt as though I was standing in the glare of powerful headlamps.

"A hundred and seventeen . . . a hundred and eighteen . . . a hundred and nineteen . . . *one hundred and twenty!*" he cried. "It's an all-time record!" He looked happier than I had ever seen him in his life. "The most my dad ever got was fifteen and he was drunk for a week afterward!" he said. "But this—this, my dear boy, is an all-time *world record!*"

"I expect it is," I said.

"And *you* did it, Danny! The whole thing was your idea in the first place!"

"I didn't do it, dad."

"Oh, yes you did! And you know what that makes you, my dear boy? It makes you the champion of the world!" He pulled up his sweater and unwound the two big cotton sacks from around his belly. "Here's yours," he said, handing one of them to me. "Fill it up quick!"

The light of the moon was so strong I could read the print across the front of the sack. J. W. CRUMP, it said, KESTON FLOUR MILLS, LONDON S.W. 17.

"You don't think that keeper with the brown teeth is watching us this very moment from behind a tree?" I said.

"No chance," my father said. "If he's anywhere, he'll be down at the filling station waiting to catch us coming home with the loot."

We started loading the pheasants into the sacks. They were soft and floppy-necked and the skin underneath the feathers was still warm.

"We can't possibly carry this lot all the way home," I said.

"Of course not. There'll be a taxi waiting for us on the track outside the wood."

"A *taxi!*" I said.

"My dad always made use of a taxi on a big job," he said.

"Why a taxi, for heaven's sake?"

"It's more secret, Danny. Nobody knows who's inside a

taxi except the driver."

"Which driver?" I asked.

"Charlie Kinch. He's only too glad to oblige."

"Does *he* know about poaching, too?"

"Old Charlie Kinch? Of course he does. He's poached more pheasants in his time than we've sold gallons of gas."

We finished loading the sacks, and my father humped his onto his shoulders. I couldn't do that with mine. It was too heavy for me. "Drag it," my father said. "Just drag it along the ground." My sack had sixty birds inside it and it weighed a ton. But it slid quite easily over the dry leaves with me walking backward and pulling it with both hands.

We came to the edge of the wood and peered through the hedge onto the track. My father said "Charlie boy" very softly, and the old man behind the wheel of the taxi poked his head out into the moonlight and gave us a sly toothless grin. We slid through the hedge, dragging the sacks after us along the ground.

"Hello hello hello," Charlie Kinch said. "What's all this?"

17

❧

The Taxi

TWO MINUTES LATER we were safely inside the taxi and cruising slowly down the bumpy track toward the road.

My father was bursting with pride and excitement. He kept leaning forward and tapping Charlie Kinch on the shoulder and saying, "How about it, Charlie? How about this for a haul?" And Charlie kept glancing back popeyed at the huge bulging sacks. "Cripes, man!" he kept saying. "How did you do it?"

"Danny did it!" my father said proudly. "My son Danny is the champion of the world."

Then Charlie said, "I reckon pheasants is going to be a bit scarce up at Mr. Victor Hazell's opening-day shoot tomorrow, eh, Willum?"

"I imagine they are, Charlie," my father said. "I imagine they are."

"All those fancy folk," Old Charlie said, "driving in from miles around in their big shiny cars, and there won't be a blinking bird anywhere for them to shoot!" Charlie Kinch started chuckling and chortling so much he nearly drove off the track.

"Dad," I said. "What on earth are you going to do with all these pheasants?"

"Share them out among our friends," my father said. "There's a dozen of them for Charlie here to start with. All right, Charlie?"

"Marvelous," Charlie said. "Terrific."

"Then there'll be a dozen for Doc Spencer. And another dozen for Enoch Samways—"

"*You don't mean Sergeant Samways?*" I gasped.

"Of course," my father said. "Enoch Samways is one of my very oldest friends."

"Enoch's a good boy," Charlie Kinch said. "He's a lovely lad."

Sergeant Enoch Samways, as I knew very well, was the village policeman. He was a huge, rather plump man with a bristly black moustache who strode up and down our High Street with the proud and measured tread of a man who knows he is in charge. The silver buttons on his uniform sparkled like diamonds, and the mere sight of him frightened

me so much I used to cross over to the other side of the street whenever he approached.

"Enoch Samways likes a piece of roasted pheasant as much as the next man," my father said.

"I reckon he knows a thing or two about catching 'em, as well," Charlie Kinch said.

I was astounded. But I was also rather pleased because now that I knew the great Sergeant Samways was human like the rest of us, perhaps I wouldn't be so scared of him in the future.

"Are you going to share them out tonight, dad?" I asked.

"Not tonight, Danny, no. You must always walk home empty-handed after a poaching trip. You can never be sure Mr. Rabbetts or one of his gang isn't waiting for you by the front door to see if you're carrying anything."

"Ah, but he's a crafty one, that Mr. Rabbetts is," Charlie Kinch said. "The best thing is to pour a pound of sugar in the gas tank of his car when he ain't looking, then he can't ever come snooping around your house later on. We always made sure to give the keepers a little sugar in their tanks before we went out on a poach. I'm surprised you didn't bother to do that, Willum, especially on a big job like this one."

"What does the sugar do?" I asked.

"Blimey, it gums up the whole ruddy works," Charlie Kinch said. "You've got to take the entire engine to pieces before it'll go again after it's had the sugar. Ain't that right, Willum?"

"That's quite right, Charlie," my father said.

We came off the bumpy track onto the main road and Charlie Kinch got the old taxicab into top gear and headed for the village.

"Are you dumping these birds at Mrs. Clipstone's place tonight?" he asked.

"Yes," my father told him. "Drive straight to Mrs. Clipstone's."

"Why Mrs. Clipstone's?" I asked. "What's she got to do with it?"

"Mrs. Clipstone delivers everyone's pheasants," my father said. "Haven't I told you that?"

"No, dad, you haven't," I said, aghast. I was now more stunned than ever. Mrs. Grace Clipstone was the wife of the Reverend Lionel Clipstone, the local vicar.

"Always choose a respectable woman to deliver your pheasants," my father announced. "That's correct, Charlie, isn't it?"

"Mrs. Clipstone's a right smart lady," Charlie said.

I could hardly believe what they were saying. It was beginning to look as though just about everybody in the entire district was in on this poaching lark.

"The vicar is very fond of roasted pheasant for his dinner," my father said.

"Who isn't?" Charlie Kinch said, and he started chuckling to himself all over again.

We were driving through the village now. The streetlights were lit and the men were wandering home from the pubs, all full of beer. I saw Mr. Snoddy, my headmaster, a bit wobbly on his feet and trying to let himself in secretly through the side door of his house. But what *he* didn't see was Mrs. Snoddy's sharp frosty face sticking out of the upstairs window, watching him.

"You know something, Danny?" my father said. "We've done these birds a great kindness putting them to sleep in this nice, painless way. They'd have had a nasty time of it tomorrow if we hadn't got to them first."

"Rotten shots, most of them fellows are," Charlie Kinch said. "At least half the birds finish up winged and wounded."

The taxi turned left and swung in through the gates of the vicarage. There were no lights in the house and nobody met us. My father and I got out and dumped the pheasants in the coal shed at the rear. Then we said good-bye to Charlie Kinch and began to walk the two miles back to the filling station.

18

❧

Home

SOON WE HAD LEFT the village behind us and were in open country. There was no one else in sight, just the two of us, my father and I, tired but happy, striding out along the curvy country road in the light of the moon.

"I can't *believe* it!" my father kept saying. "I simply cannot *believe* we pulled it off!"

"My heart is still thumping," I said.

"So is mine! So is mine! But oh, Danny," he cried, laying a hand on my shoulder, "didn't we have a glorious time!"

We were walking right in the middle of the road as though it were a private driveway running through our country estate and we were the lords of all we surveyed.

"Do you realize, Danny," my father said, "that on this very night, on this Friday the thirtieth of September, you and I have actually bagged *one hundred and twenty* prime pheasants from Mr. Victor Hazell's wood?"

I looked at my father. His face was alight with happiness and his arms were waving all over the place as he went prancing along the middle of the road with his funny iron foot going *clink, clink, clink.*

"Roasted pheasant!" he cried out, addressing the moon and the entire countryside. "The finest and most succulent dish on earth! I don't suppose you've ever eaten roasted pheasant, have you, Danny?"

"Never," I said.

"You wait!" he cried. "You just wait till you taste it! It has an unbelievable flavor! It's sheer magic!"

"Does it *have* to be roasted, dad?"

"Of course it has to be roasted. You don't ever boil a young bird. Why do you ask that?"

"I was wondering how we would do the roasting," I said. "Don't you have to have an oven or something?"

"Of course," he said.

"But we don't have an oven, dad. All we've got is a kerosene burner."

"I know," he said. "And that is why I have decided to buy an oven."

"Buy one!" I cried.

"Yes, Danny," he said. "With such a great and glorious stock of pheasants on our hands, it is important that we have the proper equipment. Therefore we shall go back into the village tomorrow morning and we shall buy an electric oven. We can get one at Wheeler's. And we'll put it in the workshop. We've got plenty of electric plugs in the workshop."

"Won't it be very expensive?"

"No expense is too great for roasted pheasant," my father announced superbly. "And don't forget, Danny, before we

put the bird in the oven, we have to lay strips of fat bacon across the breast to keep it nice and juicy. And breadsauce, too. We shall have to make breadsauce. You must never have roasted pheasant without lashings of breadsauce. There are three things you must always have with roasted pheasant— breadsauce, potato chips, and boiled parsnips."

There was half a minute's silence as we both allowed ourselves the pleasure of dreaming about these beautiful foods.

"And I'll tell you what else we've got to get," my father said. "We've got to get one of those deep freezers where you can store things for months and months and they never go rotten."

"Dad!" I said. "No!"

"But don't you realize, Danny, that even after we've given birds away to all our friends, to Charlie Kinch and the Reverend Clipstone and Doc Spencer and Enoch Samways and all the rest of them, there'll still be about fifty left for us. That is why we are going to need a deep freezer."

"But it'll cost the earth!"

"And worth every penny of it!" he cried. "Just imagine, Danny, my boy, any time we fancy a nice roasted pheasant for our supper, all we've got to do is open up the lid of the freezer and help ourselves! Kings and queens don't live any better than that!"

A barn owl flew across the road in front of us, its great white wings waving slowly in the moonlight.

"Did *your* mum have an oven in the kitchen, dad, when you were a boy?" I asked.

"She had something better than an oven," he said. "It was called a cooker. It was a great big long black thing, and we used to stoke it up with coal and keep it going for twenty-four hours a day. It never went out. And if we didn't have any coal, we used bits of wood."

"Could you roast pheasants in it?"

"You could roast anything in it, Danny. It was a lovely thing, that old cooker. It used to keep the whole house warm in the winter."

"But *you* never had a cooker of your own, did you, dad, you and mum, when you got married? Or an oven?"

"No," he said. "We couldn't afford things like that."

"Then how did you roast your pheasants?"

"Ah," he said, "that was quite a trick. We used to build a fire outside the caravan and roast them on a spit, the way the gypsies do."

"What's a spit?" I asked.

"It's just a long metal spike and you stick it through the pheasant and put it over the fire and keep turning it round. What you do is you push two forked sticks into the ground on either side of the fire and rest the spit on the forks."

"Did it roast them well?"

"Fairly well," he said. "But an oven would do it better. Listen, Danny, Mr. Wheeler has all sorts of marvelous ovens in his shop now. He's got one in there with so many dials and knobs on it, it looks like the cockpit of an airplane."

"Is that the one you want to buy, dad?"

"I don't know," he said. "We'll decide tomorrow."

We kept walking, and soon we saw the filling station glimmering in the moonlight ahead of us.

"Will Mr. Rabbetts be waiting for us, do you think, dad?" I asked.

"If he is, you won't see him, Danny. They always hide and watch you from behind a hedge or a tree and only come out if you are carrying a sack over your shoulder or if your pocket is bulging with something suspicious. We are carrying nothing at all. So don't worry about it."

Whether or not Mr. Rabbetts was watching us as we entered the filling station and headed for the caravan, I do not know. We saw no sign of him. Inside the caravan, my father lit the kerosene lamp, and I lit the burner and put the kettle on to make us a cup of cocoa each.

"That," my father said as we sat sipping our hot cocoa a few minutes later, "was the greatest time I've ever had in my whole life."

19

Rockabye Baby

AT EIGHT THIRTY THE NEXT morning my father went into the workshop and dialed Doc Spencer's number on the telephone.

"Now listen, doctor," he said. "If you could be here at the filling station in about half an hour, I think I might have a little surprise present for you." The doctor said something in reply and my father replaced the receiver.

At nine o'clock, Doc Spencer arrived in his car. My father went over to him and the two of them held a whispered conversation beside the pumps. Suddenly the tiny doctor clapped his hands together and sprang up high in the air, hooting with laughter.

"You don't mean it!" he cried. "It's not possible!" He rushed over to me and grasped my hand in his. "I do congratulate you, my dear boy!" he cried, pumping my hand up and down so fiercely it nearly came off. "What a triumph! What a miracle! What a victory! Now, why on earth didn't I think of that method myself? You are a genius, sir! Hail to thee, dear Danny, you're the champion of the world!"

"Here she comes!" my father called out, pointing down the road. "Here she comes, doctor!"

"Here who comes?" the doctor said.

"Mrs. Clipstone." He spoke the name proudly, as though he were a commander referring to his bravest officer.

The three of us stood together beside the pumps, looking down the road.

"Can't you see her?" my father asked.

Far away in the distance I could just make out a small figure advancing toward us.

"What's she pushing, dad?"

My father gave me a sly look.

"There's only one way of delivering pheasants safely," he said, "and that's under a baby. Isn't that right, doctor?"

"Under a *baby*?" Doc Spencer said.

"Of course. In a baby carriage with the baby on top."

"Fantastic!" the doctor said.

"My old dad thought that one up many years ago," my father said, "and it's never been known to fail yet."

"It's brilliant," Doc Spencer said. "Only a brilliant mind could think of a thing like that."

"He was a brilliant man," my father said. "Can you see her now, doctor? And that'll be young Christopher Clipstone sitting up in the carriage. He's a year and a half old. A lovely child."

"I birthed him," Doc Spencer said. "He weighed eight pounds three ounces."

I could just make out the small head of a baby sitting

high up in the carriage, which had its hood folded down.

"There's more than one hundred pheasants under that little nipper," my father said happily. "Just imagine it."

"You can't put a hundred pheasants in a baby carriage!" Doc Spencer said. "Don't be ridiculous!"

"You can if it's been specially made for the job," my father said. "This one is built extra long and extra wide, and it's got an extra-deep well underneath. Listen, you could push a cow around in there if you wanted to, let alone a hundred pheasants and a baby!"

"Did you make it yourself, dad?" I asked.

"More or less, Danny. You remember when I walked you to school and then went off to buy the raisins?"

"The day before yesterday," I said.

"Yes. And after that I went straight on to the vicarage and converted their baby carriage into this Special Extra-large Poacher's Model. It's a beauty, really it is. You wait till you see it. And Mrs. Clipstone says it pushes even easier than her ordinary one. She did a practice circuit with it in her backyard as soon as I'd finished it."

"Fantastic," the doctor said again. "Absolutely fantastic!"

"Normally," my father went on, "an ordinary bought

carriage is all you'd ever need. But then, no one's ever had a hundred pheasants to deliver before now."

"Where does the baby sit?" the doctor asked.

"On top, of course," my father said. "All you need is a sheet to cover them and the baby sits on the sheet. A bunch of pheasants makes a nice soft mattress for any child."

"I don't doubt it," the doctor said.

"He'll be having a very comfortable ride today, young Christopher," my father said.

We stood beside the pumps waiting for Mrs. Clipstone to arrive. It was the first of October, one of those warm windless autumn mornings with a darkening sky and a smell of thunder in the air.

What was so marvelous about my father, I thought, was the way he always surprised you. It was impossible to be with him for long without being astounded and surprised by one thing or another. He was like a conjuror bringing things out of a hat. Right now it was the carriage and the baby. In a few minutes it would be something else again, I felt sure of that.

"Right through the village, bold as brass," my father said. "Good for her."

"She seems in an awful hurry, dad," I said. "She's sort of half running. Don't you think she's sort of half running, Doctor Spencer?"

"I imagine she's just a bit anxious to unload her cargo," the doctor said.

My father squinted down the road at the approaching

figure. "She does appear to be going a bit quick, doesn't she?" he said carefully.

"She's going very quick," I said.

There was a pause. My father was beginning to stare very hard at the lady in the distance.

"Perhaps she doesn't want to be caught in the rain," he said. "I'll bet that's exactly what it is. She thinks it's going to rain and she doesn't want the baby to get wet."

"She could put the hood up," I said.

He didn't answer this.

"She's *running!*" Doc Spencer cried. "Look!"

It was true. Mrs. Clipstone had suddenly broken into a full sprint.

My father stood very still, staring at her. And in the silence that followed I fancied I could hear a baby screaming.

"What's the matter, dad?"

He didn't reply.

"There's something wrong with that baby," Doc Spencer said. "Listen."

At this point, Mrs. Clipstone was about two hundred yards away from us but closing fast.

"Can you hear him now, dad?"

"Yes, I can hear him."

"He's yelling his head off," Doc Spencer said.

The small shrill voice in the distance was growing louder every second, frantic, piercing, nonstop.

"He's having a fit," my father said. "It's a good thing we've got a doctor handy."

Doc Spencer didn't say anything.

"That's why she's running, doctor," my father said. "He's having a fit and she wants to get him in here quick and put him under a cold faucet."

"Some noise," I said.

"If it isn't a fit," my father said, "you can bet your life it's something like it."

"I doubt it's a fit," the doctor said.

My father shifted his feet uneasily on the gravel of the driveway. "There's a thousand and one different things keep happening every day to little babies like that," he said. "You know that, don't you, doctor?"

"Of course," Doc Spencer said. "Every day."

"I knew a baby once who caught his fingers in the spokes of a carriage wheel," my father said. "It cut them clean off."

The doctor smiled.

"Whatever it is," my father said, "I wish to heaven she'd stop running. It'll give the game away."

A long truck loaded with bricks came up behind the baby

carriage. The driver slowed down and poked his head out the window to stare. Mrs. Clipstone ignored him and flew on. She was so close now I could see her mouth wide open, panting for breath. I noticed she was wearing white gloves on her hands, very prim and dainty. And there was a funny little white hat to match, perched right on the top of her head, like a mushroom.

Suddenly, out of the carriage, straight up into the air, flew an enormous pheasant!

My father let out a cry of horror.

The fool in the truck started roaring with laughter.

The pheasant flapped around drunkenly for a few seconds, then it lost height and landed on the grass by the side of the road.

"Crikey!" Doc Spencer said. "Look at that!"

A grocer's van came up behind the truck and began hooting to get by. Mrs. Clipstone kept on running.

Then—WHOOSH!—a second pheasant flew up out of the carriage.

Then a third and a fourth.

"Great Scott!" Doc Spencer said. "I know what's happened! *It's the sleeping pills! They're wearing off!*"

My father didn't say a word.

Mrs. Clipstone covered the last fifty yards at a tremendous pace. She came swinging into the filling station with birds flying out of the carriage in all directions.

"What on earth's happening?" she shrieked. She pulled up sharp against the first pump and seized the screaming infant in her arms, dragging him clear.

With the weight of the child suddenly lifted away, a great cloud of pheasants rose up out of the gigantic baby carriage. There must have been well over a hundred of them, for the whole sky above us was filled with huge brown birds clapping their wings.

"A sleeping pill doesn't last forever," Doc Spencer said, shaking his head sadly. "It always wears off by the next morning."

The pheasants were too dopey to fly far. In a few seconds down they came again and settled themselves like a swarm of locusts all over the filling station. The place was covered with them. They sat wing to wing along the roof of the workshop, and about a dozen were clinging to the sill of the office window. Some had flown down on to the rack that held the bottles of lubricating oil, and others were sliding about on the hood of Doc Spencer's car. One cock with a fine tail was perched superbly on top of a gas pump, and quite a number—those that were too drunk to do anything else—simply squatted in the driveway at our feet, fluffing their feathers and blinking their small eyes.

My father stayed remarkably calm. But not poor Mrs. Clipstone. "They nearly pecked him to pieces!" she was crying, clasping the screaming baby to her bosom.

"Take him into the caravan, Mrs. Clipstone," my father said. "All these birds are making him nervous. And Danny, push that carriage into the workshop quick."

Mrs. Clipstone disappeared into our caravan with the

baby. I pushed the carriage into the workshop.

Across the road, a line of cars had already started forming behind the truck and the grocery van. People were opening their doors and getting out and beginning to cross over to stare at the pheasants.

"Watch out, dad!" I said. "Look who's here!"

20

Good-bye Mr. Hazell

THE BIG, SHINY SILVER Rolls-Royce had braked suddenly and come to a stop right alongside the filling station. Behind the wheel I could see the enormous pink beery face of Mr. Victor Hazell staring at the pheasants. I could see the mouth hanging open, the eyes bulging out of his head like toadstools, and the skin of his face turning from pink to bright scarlet. The car door opened and out he came, resplendent in fawn-colored riding breeches and high polished boots. There was a yellow silk scarf around his neck with red dots on it, and he had a sort of bowler hat on his head. The great shooting party was about to begin, and he was on his way to greet the guests.

He left the door of the Rolls open and came at us like a charging bull. My father, Doc Spencer, and I stood close together in a little group, waiting for him. He started shouting at us the moment he got out of the car, and he went on shouting for a long time after that. I am sure you would like to know what he said, but I cannot possibly repeat it here. The language he used was so foul and filthy it scorched my earholes. Words came out of his mouth that I had never heard before and hope never to hear again. Little flecks of white foam began forming around his lips and running down his chin onto the yellow silk scarf.

I glanced at my father. He was standing very still and very calm, waiting for the shouting to finish. The color was back in his cheeks now, and I could see the tiny twinkling wrinkles of a smile around the corners of his eyes.

Doc Spencer stood beside him. He also was very calm. He was looking at Mr. Hazell rather as one would look at a slug on a leaf of lettuce in the salad.

I myself did not feel quite so calm.

"But they are *not* your pheasants," my father said at last. "They're mine."

"Don't lie to me, man!" yelled Mr. Hazell. "I'm the only person around here who has pheasants!"

"They are on my land," my father said quietly. "They

flew onto my land, and so long as they stay on my land they belong to me. Don't you know the rules, you bloated old blue-faced baboon?"

Doc Spencer started to giggle. Mr. Hazell's skin turned from scarlet to purple. His eyes and his cheeks were bulging so much with rage it looked as though someone was blowing up his face with a pump. He glared at my father. Then he glared around at the dopey pheasants swarming all over the filling station. "What's the matter with 'em?" he shouted. "What've you done to 'em?"

At this point, pedaling grandly toward us on his black bicycle, came the arm of the law in the shape of Sergeant Enoch Samways, resplendent in his blue uniform and shiny silver buttons. It was always a mystery to me how Sergeant Samways could sniff out trouble wherever it was. Let there be a few boys fighting on the sidewalk, or two motorists arguing over a dented fender, and you could bet your life the village policeman would be there within minutes.

We all saw him coming now, and a little hush fell upon the entire company. I imagine the same sort of thing happens when a king or a president enters a room full of chattering people. They all stop talking and stand very still as a mark of respect for a powerful and important person.

Sergeant Samways dismounted from his bicycle and threaded his way carefully through the mass of pheasants squatting on the ground. The face behind the big black moustache showed no surprise, no anger, no emotion of any

kind. It was calm and neutral, as the face of the law should always be.

For a full half minute he allowed his eyes to travel slowly around the filling station, gazing at the mass of pheasants squatting all over the place. The rest of us, including even Mr. Hazell, waited in silence for judgment to be pronounced.

"Well, well, well," said Sergeant Samways at last, puffing out his chest and addressing nobody in particular. "What, may I hask, is 'appenin' around 'ere?" Sergeant Samways had a funny habit of sometimes putting the letter *h* in front of words that shouldn't have an *h* there at all. And as though to balance things out, he would take away the *h* from words that should have begun with that letter.

"I'll tell you what's happening around here!" shouted Mr. Hazell, advancing upon the policeman. "These are *my pheasants*, and this rogue," pointing at my father, "has enticed them out of my woods onto his filthy little filling station!"

"*Hen*-ticed?" said Sergeant Samways, looking first at Mr. Hazell, then at us. "*Hen*-ticed them, did you say?"

"Of course he enticed them!"

"Well now," said the sergeant, propping his bicycle carefully against one of our pumps. "This is a very hinterestin' haccusation, very hinterestin' indeed, because I hain't never 'eard of nobody *hen*-ticin' a pheasant across six miles of fields and open countryside. 'Ow do you think this *hen*-ticin' was performed, Mr. 'Azell, if I may hask?"

"Don't ask me *how* he did it because I don't know!" shouted Mr. Hazell. "But he's done it all right! The proof is all around you! All my finest birds are sitting here in this dirty little filling station when they ought to be up in my own wood getting ready for the shoot!" The words poured out of Mr. Hazell's mouth like hot lava from an erupting volcano.

"Am I correct," said Sergeant Samways, "am I habsolutely haccurate in thinkin' that today is the day of your great shootin' party, Mr. 'Azell?"

"That's the whole point!" cried Mr. Hazell, stabbing his

forefinger into the sergeant's chest as though he were punching a typewriter or an adding machine. "And if I don't get these birds back on my land quick sharp, some very important people are going to be extremely angry this morning. And one of my guests, I'll have you know, sergeant, is none other than your own boss, the Lord Chief Constable of the County! So you had better do something about it fast, hadn't you, unless you want to lose those sergeant's stripes of yours!"

Sergeant Samways did not like people poking their fingers in his chest, least of all Mr. Hazell, and he showed it by twitching his upper lip so violently that his moustache came alive and jumped about like some small, bristly animal.

"Now just one minute," he said to Mr. Hazell. "Just one minute, please. Am I to understand that you are haccusin' this gentleman of committin' this hact?"

"Of course I am!" cried Mr. Hazell. "I know he did it!"

"And do you 'ave any hevidence to support this haccusation?"

"The evidence is all around you!" shouted Mr. Hazell. "Are you blind or something?"

Now my father stepped forward. He took one small pace

to the front and fixed Mr. Hazell with his marvelously bright twinkly eyes. "Surely you know how these pheasants came here?" he said softly.

"Surely I do *not* know how they came here!" snapped Mr. Hazell.

"Then I shall tell you," my father said, "because it is quite simple, really. They all knew they were going to be shot today if they stayed in your wood, so they flew in here to wait until the shooting was over."

"Rubbish!" yelled Mr. Hazell.

"It's not rubbish at all," my father said. "They are extremely intelligent birds, pheasants. Isn't that so, doctor?"

"They have tremendous brainpower," Doc Spencer said. "They know exactly what's going on."

"It would undoubtedly be a great honor," my father said, "to be shot by the Lord Chief Constable of the County, and an even greater one to be eaten afterward by Lord Thistlethwaite, but I do not think a pheasant would see it that way."

"You are scoundrels, both of you!" shouted Mr. Hazell. "You are rapscallions of the worst kind!"

"Now then, now then," said Sergeant Samways. "Hinsults ain't going to get us nowhere. They only haggravate things. Therefore, gentlemen, I 'ave a suggestion to put before you. I suggest that we all of us make a big heffort to drive these birds back over the road onto Mr. 'Azell's land. 'Ow does that strike you, Mr. 'Azell?"

"It'll be a step in the right direction," Mr. Hazell said. "Get on with it, then."

" 'Ow about you, Willum?" the sergeant said to my father. "Are you agreeable to this haction?"

"I think it's a fine idea," my father said, giving Sergeant Samways one of his funny looks. "I'll be very glad to help. So will Danny."

What's he up to now? I wondered, because whenever my father gave somebody one of his funny looks, it meant something funny was going to happen. And Sergeant Samways, I noticed, also had quite a sparkle in his usually stern eye. "Come on, my lads!" he cried. "Let's push these lazy birds over the road!" And with that he began striding around the filling station, waving his arms at the pheasants and shouting "Shoo! Shoo! Off you go! Beat it! Get out of 'ere!"

My father and I joined him in this rather absurd exercise, and for the second time that morning clouds of pheasants rose up into the air, clapping their enormous wings. It was then I realized that in order to fly across the road, the birds would first have to fly over Mr. Hazell's mighty Rolls-Royce, which lay right in their path with its one door still open. Most of the pheasants were too dopey to manage this, so down they came again, smack on top of the great silver automobile. They were all over the roof and the hood, sliding and slithering and trying to keep a grip on that beautifully polished surface. I could hear their sharp claws scraping into the paintwork as they struggled to hang on, and already they were depositing their filthy droppings all over the roof.

"Get them off!" screamed Mr. Hazell. "Get them away!"

"Don't you worry, Mr. 'Azell, sir," Sergeant Samways cried

out. "We'll fix 'em for you. Come on, boys! Heasy does it. Shoo 'em right over the road!"

"Not on my car, you idiot!" Mr. Hazell bellowed, jumping up and down. "Send them the other way!"

"We will, sir, we will!" answered Sergeant Samways.

In less than a minute, the Rolls was literally festooned with pheasants, all scratching and scrabbling and making their disgusting runny messes over the shiny silver paint. What is more, I saw at least a dozen of them fly right *inside* the car through the open door by the driver's seat. Whether or not Sergeant Samways had cunningly steered them in there himself, I didn't know, but it happened so quickly that Mr. Hazell never even noticed.

"Get these birds off my car!" Mr. Hazell bellowed. "Can't you see they're ruining the paintwork, you madman!"

"Paintwork?" Sergeant Samways said. "What paintwork?" He had stopped chasing the pheasants now and he stood there looking at Mr. Hazell and shaking his head sadly from side to side. "We've done our very best to hencourage these birds over the road," he said, "but it ain't worked."

"My car, man!" shouted Mr. Hazell. "Get them away from my car!"

"Ah," the sergeant said. "Your car. Yes, I see what you mean, sir. Beastly dirty birds, pheasants are. But why don't you just 'op in quick and drive 'er away fast? They'll 'ave to get off then, won't they?"

Mr. Hazell, who seemed only too glad of an excuse to escape from this madhouse, made a dash for the open door of the Rolls and leaped into the driver's seat. The moment he was in, Sergeant Samways slammed the door, and suddenly there was the most infernal uproar inside the car as a dozen or more enormous pheasants started squawking and flapping all over the seats and around Mr. Hazell's head. "Drive on, Mr. 'Azell, sir!" shouted Sergeant Samways through the window in his most commanding policeman's voice. "'Urry up, 'urry up, 'urry up! Get goin' quick! Hignore them pheasants, Mr. 'Azell, and haccelerate that hengine!"

Mr. Hazell didn't have much choice. He had to make a run for it now. He started the motor, and the great Rolls shot off down the road with clouds of pheasants rising up from it in all directions.

Then an extraordinary thing happened. The pheasants that had flown up off the car *stayed up in the air*. They didn't come flapping drunkenly down as we had expected them to. They stayed up and kept on flying. Over the top of the filling station they flew, and over the caravan, and over the field at the back where our little outdoor lavatory stood, and over the next field, and over the crest of the hill—until they disappeared from sight.

"Great Scott!" Doc Spencer cried. "Just look at that! They've recovered! The sleeping pills have worn off at last!"

Now all the other pheasants around the place were beginning to come awake. They were standing up tall on their legs and ruffling their feathers and turning their heads quickly from side to side. One or two of them started running about, then all the others started running; and when Sergeant Samways flapped his arms at them, the whole lot took off into the air and flew over the filling station and were gone.

Suddenly, there was not a pheasant left. And it was very interesting to see that none of them had flown across the road, or even down the road in the direction of Hazell's Wood and the great shooting party. Every one of them had flown in exactly the opposite direction!

21

*

Doc Spencer's Surprise

ALONG THE ROAD, a line of about twenty automobiles and trucks was parked bumper to bumper, and people were standing about in groups, laughing and talking about the astonishing sight they had just witnessed.

"Come along, now!" Sergeant Samways called out, striding toward them. "Get goin'! Get movin'! We can't 'ave this! You're blockin' the 'ighway!"

Nobody ever disobeyed Sergeant Samways, and soon the people were drifting back to their automobiles. In a few minutes, they, too, were all gone. Only the four of us were left now—Doc Spencer, Sergeant Samways, my father, and me.

"Well, Willum," Sergeant Samways said, coming back from the road to join us beside the pumps. "Them pheasants was the most hastonishin' sight I ever seed in my hentire life!"

"It was lovely," Doc Spencer said. "Just lovely. Didn't you enjoy it, Danny?"

"Marvelous," I said.

"Pity we lost them," my father said. "It very nearly broke my heart when they all started flying out of the carriage. I knew we'd lost them then."

"But 'ow in 'eaven's name did you ever catch 'em in the first place?" asked Sergeant Samways. " 'Ow did you do it, Willum? Come on, man. Let me in on the secret."

My father told him. He kept it short, but even then it made a fine story. And all the way through it, the sergeant kept saying, "Well, I never! Well, I'll be blowed! You could knock me down with a feather! Stone the crows!" and things like that. And when the story was finished, he pointed his long policeman's finger straight at my face and cried, "Well, I'll be jiggered! I never would 'ave thought a little nipper like you could come up with such a fantastical brainwave as that! Young man, I congratulate you!"

"He'll go a long way, young Danny will, you see if he doesn't," Doc Spencer said. "He'll be a great inventor one day."

To be spoken about like that by the two men I admired most in the world after my father, made me blush and stutter.

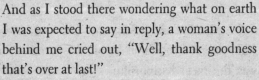

And as I stood there wondering what on earth I was expected to say in reply, a woman's voice behind me cried out, "Well, thank goodness that's over at last!"

This, of course, was Mrs. Grace Clipstone, who was now picking her way cautiously down the caravan steps with young Christopher in her arms. "Never in my life," she was saying, "have I seen such a shambles as that!"

The little white hat was still perched on the top of her head, and the white gloves were still on her hands. "What a gathering!" she said, advancing toward us. "What a gathering we have here of rogues and varmints! Good morning, Enoch."

"Good morning to you, Mrs. Clipstone," Sergeant Samways said.

"How's the baby?" my father asked her.

"The baby is better, thank you, William," she said. "Though I doubt he'll ever be quite the same again."

"Of course he will," Doc Spencer said. "Babies are tough."

"I don't care how tough they are!" she answered. "How would *you* like it if you were being taken for a nice quiet walk in your baby carriage on a pretty autumn morning— and you were sitting on a lovely soft mattress—and suddenly the mattress comes alive and starts bouncing you up and down like a stormy sea—and the next thing you know, there's about a hundred sharp curvy beaks poking up from underneath the mattress and pecking you to pieces!"

The doctor cocked his head over to one side, then to the other, and smiled at Mrs. Clipstone.

"So you think it's funny?" she cried. "Well just you wait, Doctor Spencer, and one night I'll put a few snakes or crocodiles or something under *your* mattress and see how you like it!"

Sergeant Samways was fetching his bicycle from beside the pumps. "Well, ladies and gents," he said. "I must be off and see who else is gettin' into mischief around 'ere."

"I am truly sorry you were troubled, Enoch," my father said. "And thanks very much indeed for the help."

"I wouldn't 'ave missed this one for all the tea in China," Sergeant Samways said. "But it did sadden me most terrible, Willum, to see all those lovely birds go slippin' right through our fingers like that. Because to my mind, there don't hexist a more luscious dish than roasted pheasant anywhere on this earth."

"It's going to sadden the vicar a lot more than it saddens you," said Mrs. Clipstone. "That's all he's been talking about ever since he got out of bed this morning, the lovely roasted pheasant he's going to have for his dinner tonight."

"He'll get over it," Doc Spencer said.

"He will not get over it and it's a beastly shame!" Mrs. Clipstone said. "Because now all I've got to give him are some awful frozen fillets of codfish."

"But," my father said, "surely you didn't load *all* those pheasants into the carriage, did you? You were meant to keep at least a dozen for you and the vicar!"

"Oh, I know that," she wailed. "But I was so tickled at the thought of strolling calmly through the village with Christopher sitting on a hundred and twenty birds, I simply forgot to keep any back for ourselves. And now, alas, they're all gone! And so is the vicar's supper!"

The doctor went over to Mrs. Clipstone and took her by the arm. "You come with me, Grace," he said. "I've got something to show you." He led her across to my father's workshop where the big doors stood wide open.

The rest of us stayed where we were and waited.

"Good grief! Come and look at this!" Mrs. Clipstone called out from inside the workshop. "William! Enoch! Danny! Come and look!"

We hurried over and entered the workshop.

It was a great sight.

Laid out on my father's bench amid the spanners and wrenches and oily rags were six magnificent pheasants, three cocks and three hens.

"There we are, ladies and gentlemen," said the doctor, his small wrinkled face beaming with delight. "How's that?"

We were speechless.

"Two for you, Grace, to keep the vicar in a good mood," Doc Spencer said. "Two for Enoch for all the fine work he did this morning. And two for William and Danny who deserve them most of all."

"What about you, doctor?" my father asked. "That doesn't leave any for you."

"My wife has enough to do without plucking pheasants all day long," he said. "And anyway, who got them out of the woods in the first place? You and Danny."

"But how on earth did *you* get them?" my father asked him. "When did you nab them?"

"I didn't nab them," the doctor said. "I had a hunch."

"What sort of a hunch?" my father asked.

"It seemed fairly obvious," the doctor said, "that *some* of those pheasants must have gobbled up more than one raisin each. Some, if they were quick enough, might have swallowed half a dozen each, or even more. In which case they would have gotten a very heavy overdose of sleeping pills and wouldn't *ever* wake up."

"Ah-ha!" we cried. "Of course! Of course!"

"So while you were all so busy driving the birds onto old Hazell's Rolls-Royce, I sneaked in here and had a look under the sheet in the bottom of the carriage. And there they were!"

"Ham-azin!" Sergeant Samways said. "Habsolutely ha-mazin!"

"Those were the greedy ones," the doctor said. "It never pays to eat more than your fair share."

"Marvelous!" my father said. "Well done, sir!"

"Now come along, Grace," the doctor said. "I'll drive you home. You can leave this crazy baby carriage where it is. And Enoch, we'll take your birds with us and drop them off at your house on the way. We can't have the arm of the law cycling through the village with a brace of pheasants slung over his handlebars, can we?"

"I am very much hobliged to you, doctor," Sergeant Samways said. "I really am."

"Oh, you lovely man!" cried Mrs. Clipstone, flinging an arm around the tiny doctor and giving him a kiss on the cheek.

My father and I loaded four of the pheasants into the doctor's car. Mrs. Clipstone got into the front seat with the baby and the doctor sat himself behind the wheel. "Don't be sad, William," he said to my father through the window as he drove off. "It was a famous victory!"

Then Sergeant Samways mounted his bicycle and waved us good-bye and pedaled away down the road in the direction of the village. He pedaled slowly, and there was a certain majesty in the way he held himself, his head high and his back very straight, as though he were riding a fine thoroughbred mare instead of an old black bike.

22

My Father

IT WAS ALL OVER NOW. My father and I stood alone just outside the workshop, and suddenly the old place seemed to have become very quiet.

"Well, Danny," my father said, looking at me with those twinkly eyes of his, "that's that."

"It was fun, dad."

"I know it was," he said.

"I really loved it," I said.

"So did I, Danny."

He placed one hand on my shoulder and we began walking slowly toward the caravan.

"Maybe we should lock the pumps and take a holiday for the rest of the day," he said.

"You mean not open up at all?"

"Why should we?" he said. "After all, it's Saturday, isn't it?"

"But we always stay open Saturdays, dad. And Sundays."

"Maybe it's time we didn't," he said. "We could do something else instead. Something more interesting."

I waited, wondering what was coming next.

When we reached the caravan, my father climbed the steps and sat down on the little outside platform. He allowed both his legs, the plaster one and the good one, to dangle over the edge. I climbed up and sat down beside him with my feet on the steps of the ladder.

It was a fine place to sit, the platform of the caravan. It was such a quiet comfortable place to sit and talk and do nothing in pleasant weather. People with houses have a front porch or a terrace instead, with big chairs to lounge in, but I wouldn't have traded either of those for our wooden platform.

"I know a place about three miles away," my father was saying, "over Cobblers Hill and down the other side, where there's a small wood of larch trees. It is a very quiet place and the stream runs right through it."

"The stream?" I said.

He nodded and gave me another of his twinkly looks. "It's full of trout," he said.

"Oh, *could we?*" I cried. "Could we go there, dad?"

"Why not?" he said. "We could try tickling them the way Doc Spencer told us."

"Will you teach me?" I said.

"I haven't had much practice with trout," he told me. "Pheasants are more in my line. But we could always learn."

"Can we go now?" I asked, getting excited all over again.

"I thought we would just pop into the village first and buy the electric oven," he said. "You haven't forgotten about the electric oven, have you?"

"But dad," I said, "that was when we thought we were

going to have lots and lots of pheasants to roast."

"We've still got the two the Doc gave us," he said. "And with any luck we'll have lots more of them as the weeks go by. It's time we had an oven anyway. Then we can roast things properly instead of heating up baked beans in a saucepan. We could have roasted pork one day, and then if we felt like it, we could have roasted leg of lamb the next time or even roasted beef. Wouldn't you like that?"

"Yes," I said. "Of course I would. And, dad, would you be able to make your favorite thing of all?"

"What's that?" he asked.

"Toad-in-the-hole," I said.

"By golly!" he cried. "That'll be the very first thing we'll make in our new oven! Toad-in-the-hole! I'll make it in an enormous pan, the same as my old mum, with the Yorkshire pudding very crisp and raised up in huge bubbly mountains and the sausages nestling in between the mountains!"

"Can we get it today, dad? Will they deliver it at once?"

"They might, Danny. We'll have to see."

"Couldn't we order it now on the telephone?"

"We mustn't do that," my father said. "We must go personally to see Mr. Wheeler and inspect all the different models with great care."

"All right," I said. "Let's go." I was really steamed up now about getting an oven and being able to have Toad-in-the-hole and roasted pork and things like that. I couldn't wait.

My father got to his feet. "And when we've done that," he said, "we'll go off to the stream and see if we can't find us some big rainbow trout. We could take some sandwiches with us for lunch and eat them beside the stream. That will make a good day of it."

A few minutes later, the two of us were walking down the well-known road toward the village to buy the oven. My father's iron foot went *clink clink* on the hard surface and overhead some big black thunderclouds were moving slowly down the valley.

"Dad," I said.

"Yes, my love?"

"When we have our roasted pheasant supper with our new oven, do you think we could invite Doctor Spencer and Mrs. Spencer to eat it with us?"

"Great heavens!" my father cried. "What a wonderful thought! What a beautiful idea! We'll give a dinner party in their honor!"

"The only thing is," I said, "will there be enough room in the caravan for four people?"

"I think so," he said. "Just."

"But we've only got two chairs."

"That's no problem, Danny. You and I can sit on boxes." There was a short silence, then he said, "But I'll tell you what we must have and that's a tablecloth. We can't serve dinner to the doctor and his wife without a tablecloth."

"But we don't have a tablecloth, dad."

"Don't you worry about it," my father said. "We can use a sheet from one of the bunks. That's all a tablecloth is, a sort of sheet."

"What about knives and forks?" I asked.

"How many do we have?"

"Just two knives," I said, "and two forks. And those are all a bit dented."

"We shall buy two more of each," my father said. "We shall give our guests the new ones and use the old ones ourselves."

"Good," I said. "Lovely." I reached out and slid my hand into his. He folded his long fingers around my fist and held it tight, and we walked on toward the village where soon the two of us would be inspecting all the different ovens with great care and talking to Mr. Wheeler personally about them.

And after that, we would walk home again and make up some sandwiches for our lunch.

And after that, we would set off with the sandwiches in our pockets, striding up over Cobblers Hill and down the other side to the small wood of larch trees that had the stream running through it.

And after that?

Perhaps a big rainbow trout.

And after that?

There would be something else after that.

And after that?

Ah yes, and something else again.

Because what I am trying to tell you . . .

What I have been trying so hard to tell you all along is simply that my father, without the slightest doubt, was the most marvelous and exciting father any boy ever had.

≫→ **A MESSAGE** ←«

To Children Who Have Read This Book

When **you** grow up
and have children of your own,
do **please** remember something **important.**

A STODGY parent is *no fun at all!*

What a child *wants*
—and DESERVES—
is a parent who is

SPARKY!

ABOUT THE AUTHOR

ROALD DAHL's books for children include *James and the Giant Peach, Charlie and the Great Glass Elevator, Danny The Champion of the World, Fantastic Mr. Fox,* and of course the great and glorious *Charlie and the Chocolate Factory.* Mr. Dahl lives in Buckinghamshire, England.

ABOUT THE ILLUSTRATOR

JILL BENNETT got her start as an artist in the theater, designing stage sets, and it was not until her childen were nearly grown that she began to illustrate children's books. She lives with her family in Putney, on the outskirts of London, where her housetop overlooks the River Thames.

Bantam Skylark Paperbacks
The Kid-Pleasers

Especially designed for easy reading with large type, wide margins and captivating illustrations, Skylarks are "kid-pleasing" paperbacks featuring the authors, subjects and characters children love.

☐	15258	BANANA BLITZ Florence Parry Heide	$2.25
☐	15259	FREAKY FILLINS #1 David Hartley	$1.95
☐	15250	THE GOOD-GUY CAKE Barbara Dillion	$1.95
☐	15239	C.L.U.T.Z. Marilyn Wilkes	$1.95
☐	15237	MUSTARD Charlotte Graeber	$1.95
☐	15157	ALVIN FERNALD: TV ANCHORMAN Clifford Hicks	$1.95
☐	15253	ANASTASIA KRUPNIK Lois Lowry	$2.25
☐	15168	HUGH PINE Janwillen Van de Wetering	$1.95
☐	15188	DON'T BE MAD IVY Christine McDonnell	$1.95
☐	15248	CHARLIE AND THE CHOCOLATE FACTORY Roald Dahl	$2.50
☐	15174	CHARLIE AND THE GREAT GLASS ELEVATOR Roald Dahl	$2.25
☐	15165	JAMES AND THE GIANT PEACH Roald Dahl	$2.75
☐	15060	ABEL'S ISLAND William Steig	$1.95
☐	15194	BIG RED Jim Kjelgaard	$2.50
☐	15206	IRISH RED: SON OF BIG RED Jim Kjelgaard	$2.25
☐	01803	JACOB TWO-TWO MEETS THE HOODED FANG Mordecai Richler	$2.95
☐	15065	TUCK EVERLASTING Natalie Babbitt	$1.95
☐	15268	THE TWITS Roald Dahl	$2.25

Prices and availability subject to change without notice.

Buy them at your local bookstore or use this handy coupon for ordering: